Jim Anthony
Super-Detective

Volume Five

AIRSHIP 27 PRODUCTIONS

Jim Anthony: Super-Detective Volume 5
"Mastermind" © 2017 Adam Mudman Bezecny

An Airship 27 Production
www.airship27.com
www.airship27hangar.com

Interior illustrations © 2017 Richard Jun
Cover illustration © 2017 Adam Benet Shaw

Editor: Ron Fortier
Associate Editor:
Marketing and promotions manager: Michael Vance
Production and design: Rob Davis.

ISBN-10: 1-946183-22-9
ISBN-13: 978-1-946183-22-4

Printed in the United States of America

10 9 8 7 6 5 4 3 2 1

JIM ANTHONY SUPER-DETECTIVE
vs.
MASTERMIND
by Adam Mudman Bezecny

A FOUR-PART NOVEL

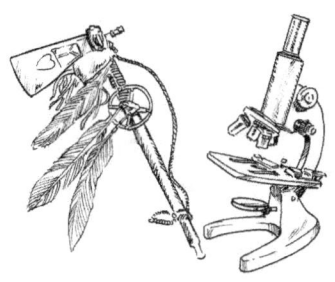

GREEK FIRE RETURNS

Theodore Sherman, chief executive of one of the greatest businesses in the world, was thankful at last for a change in pace. Unlike an unfortunate number of his wealthy friends, he was never content to just go on vacation while his board ran his business for him. Being in charge of Sherman Financial was hardly something he took lightly. However, even on leave, he held himself to a strict and professional standard of living, and that meant working at any and all hours. Also unlike his fellow businessmen, he kept no servants, and was also a lifelong bachelor, and therefore was in the midst of cooking a meal for himself. It had been a long time since he'd done so, and he was thankful no one else was in the house—he had already burnt the steak! Even with the mashed potatoes being just as he liked, he mourned this steak. And yet he seemed to remember he had another one in the old General Electric Monitor-Top in the kitchen of the west wing, so perhaps all wasn't lost. He left this kitchen at once to go look into it.

As he walked down the hallway, he didn't eyes gazing out from the darkness of one of the rooms he passed—eyes that blazed with an almost supernatural hatred. Nor did he hear any noise from the steps the possessor of these took to creep closer to the abandoned kitchen.

When the businessman returned, he wore a smile on his face. He couldn't find the steak at first but did find an excellent side of lamb which he hadn't finished from the catering at last week's finance meeting. It would be easy enough to reheat, and so his meal would be done before the potatoes got cold. Why he'd started on the potatoes first, he had no idea—but again, it *had* been awhile since he'd cooked.

Once the lamb was reheated, he remembered that he'd set out a plate of corn for a reason. His doctor *had* been telling him to keep on his vegetables, after all! He figured he could fry it in the lamb grease to give it just a little extra flavor. No chef was he—his arena of choice was that of stock brokering and loans. But he knew that the taste of lamb was irresistible, and it would make the vegetables go down a little easier.

He threw the corn into the skillet and watched the fat simmering around it. No need to let it sit in there for too long, he figured.

But there seemed at once to be a tiny light buried amidst the corn. It glowed red rather like an ember from a dying fire. Sherman turned off what

5

very little heat he was using, wondering if he had started burning it. But even as the heat of the stove faded away, the glow only became more and more intense.

Suddenly, tongues of flame shot forth from the skillet, and Sherman dodged back. "What in God's name...!" he cried out, his voice cracking at once from fear.

There was another pulse of flame, this time not confined to mere ribbons whipping out. For the last remaining moment that Sherman remained alive, he compared the wall of fire to the Lake of such in the deepest reaches of Hell.

The flames burned briefly, and though some of the wood paneling around the stove had small residual fires, by and large the only signs that there had been a fire at all were in the scorch marks around where the skillet had been heated—and, of course, the charred form crumpled on the ground, which was all that remained of the executive of Sherman Financial.

Yet there was also another sign that something weird and horrible had taken place. One which the perpetrator couldn't wait to share with the police.

Once the last remnants of the fire's roar, and Sherman's screams, had died down, the kitchen didn't stay silent for long. Slow, cautious footsteps began to make their quiet echoes on the exquisite tile of the floor. Yet the maker of these footsteps had worn these cushioned sandals specifically to avoid noise—only in this absolute dead silence could he be heard.

The footstep-maker was clad in what looked to be a scarlet toga. His hands were covered in maroon gloves, one of which was busy putting—something—back into a pocket within the toga. All around his head was a vermillion cowl that pressed tight against his face, but wasn't so tight as to reveal any of his features. Indeed, if it weren't for the traces of beard around the cruel, sneering mouth, it would be impossible to divine the gender of this fantastically-garbed intruder. Even though stealth was no longer necessary, the intruder decided it would be best to save his celebratory laugh for when he returned to his base of operations.

Just outside of the kitchen was Sherman's telephone. The invader dialed the police and began to speak.

"Don't say anything at all," he began, in a hissing whisper. "This is the Flame Wizard. I have just taken my revenge on Theodore Sherman, the corporate executive. If you wish to see for yourself, come to his mansion— his *unearned* mansion—and you'll find what's left of him. Let me just say

that I hope you bring both your appetite for cooked meat, and an ice axe."
As he hung up, he suddenly found himself unable to wait for a return
home, and a sick, high-pitched giggle rippled through the empty manor.

The police arrived ten minutes later, and by then the warlock was gone.
The officers in question, Charlie and Jack, slowly tracked the smell of burnt
meat to the kitchen. Jack gave an indistinct scream, while Charlie crossed
himself and offered a prayer to Mary Above.

"My God, Charlie," Jack said, once he regained his facilities of speech.
"Who could've...?"

Charlie was distracted by something else entirely, and Jack kicked himself when he realized he hadn't noticed it. Admittedly, even with his experience as a cop, finding something like *this* was still a matter of complete and utter horror. But obvious enough was the fact that the stove, and
much of the area around it, was covered in a sheath of *ice*.

The question of "who could've done this" became less of a questioning
of the sick nature of the murderer and more about the sort of mastery of
some unknown art that could incinerate a man, and yet also create patches of the coldest ice.

Of course, when both of the cops gave their report to their chief, the
answer—or the chance for an answer—was obvious enough. They had to
call Jim Anthony, the Super-Detective, for only his own virtuoso standing
in the ways of science could solve this grim mystery!

• • •

"Holy Gee-man-ee, Jim," a voice at the head of the car said. The words
weren't spoken as if they were supposed to be followed up by something—
they were more an indication of remorse. The carrier of those words was
Tom Gentry, chauffeur, pilot, and general right-hand man of the famous
Jim Anthony. Jim, from the backseat, currently shared Tom's solemn tone.
But he shared it silently, for he was deep in thought. Officers Jack and
Charlie had relayed the nature of the crime to him in great detail, once
they'd regained their senses. But to what he expected to be their disappointment, he hadn't been able to conjure any answers until he saw the
scene himself. And, he admitted, it was indeed very baffling—maybe even
sight wouldn't be able to aid him.

He sensed in Tom's voice, however, that that admission had been the
wrong thing for him to say—he should have remained brave and resolute,
a figure of authority, as was expected from him at this point. That was

his sense of responsibility. It had been instilled in him by his grandfather, Mephito, who had been his guide in his current path in life. Mephito's daughter, Fawn Johntom, had also been a great influence. She gave an additional inheritance, however—a sixth sense that would feel for danger. It was all ablaze now, and sometimes Jim felt it was a distraction, as his science was ill-informed at providing an explanation for it. Most of the time, however, his iron will could repress any distraction.

Yet still he was stumped by the weird events that had taken place at the old house of Theodore Sherman!

Fortunately, Tom Gentry's voice once again broke the silence.

"We're here, Jim. You want me to stay at the car?"

Jim managed a faint smile as his trance was broken. "Come with me, Tom. I think it'd do some good to put two heads together."

"As the saying goes, eh, Jim?"

Anthony said nothing in response as both he and his chauffeur climbed from the car. Ahead was the awe-inspiring hulk of Sherman Manor. Hulk indeed was a good word for it, for it was little else now, and certainly not a home—as a bachelor Sherman left no heirs, and of course having no servants, left them nothing either. For now it was the property of New York State, while his company was left to have a say in how his wealth should be distributed. But the police, of course, had free reign on the scene, and with them came the authority of Jim Anthony.

The chief of police approached him, and shook his hand heartily. "Nice to see you again, Anthony," he said. "Even if most of what I've seen of you is usually in the papers these days."

"I don't go out of my way to cause headlines," Anthony said slyly. "I'd like to be directed at once to the kitchen, please."

The police were sometimes staggered a little by Anthony's directness, but their shock didn't make them forget the importance of what was taking place here. A group of cops led Anthony and Tom down into where the crime had taken place. The body had been mercifully covered with a sheet, and Anthony was able to spray deodorants in the air that helped everyone breathe a little easier.

He was in the process of approaching the stove in the middle of the crime scene, where a nudge from Tom pointed him in the direction of someone who was standing alongside the rest of the police squad. He knew better enough not to say anything, and Anthony knew better not to emote. Even if the figure Tom had pointed to him had spawned a low reaction in him.

She had copper red hair. That was the first thing that caught his eye—but slowly, he saw more of her. The hair seemed to flow straight into the crimson of her dress, which seemed even to Anthony's eyes to go on forever. And as a shape extending from the curve of her hair was the oval of her lips. But the symmetry of color was only a surface detail, as when Anthony's sharp eyes focused (and he admittedly found it difficult to focus) he saw a face around those lips that reflected great intelligence. Her face seemed taut as if she was trying to solve the case herself, though she was focused on her job, which seemed to be a photographer for the coroner's office (at least so he deduced). Eventually, they both realized they were staring at each other.

Jim looked away, and returned his gaze instead to the stove. Already he was discerning some important facts: that the oven itself was not the source of the explosion—and that whatever had erupted into flames had been above or shielded from the stove in some way. It must have been something in a now all-but-vaporized skillet that tricked it off.

"The bomb was planted somewhere in his food," Jim said then.

"Lord, Jim," Tom cut in. "Tampering with his food? That's certainly a low blow."

"But an effective one, Tom. Whatever it was that did this—that created such an explosion—must have been small."

"Mr. Anthony, sir—where did the ice come from, then?" one of the officers said.

Jim sorted out his words carefully. "I think the explosion was different from what we're used to—most explosions, as you know, are usually hottest at the source. But this element, when added to even low heat, could possible create a field of thermal magnetism—as I'll call it for now, at least—that would suck thermal energy out of nearby sources and create a shell of flames."

"Something that surely can't exist," the same officer said. But Anthony shook his head.

"The image is triggering memories in my mind that have a lot of parallels to this case. For now, I'm going to tell you as a chemist that there are many reactions possible, some indeed very fantastic. Actually, I want to look up a chemical detail that I just remembered." He crouched low to the burnt ruin of the oven and closed his eyes. "I'm going to spend a few seconds trying to work on that memory. Tom, could you check the refrigerator for me, please?"

Tom lightly gulped. "The refrigerator, Jim?"

"Yeah. Just take a look."

Tom opened it up, and there was none of the usual fog coming out of it, like when Dawkins the butler opened up their own fridge when he and Jim had some downtime at the Penthouse. He then noticed there wasn't any cold coming out of it either, nor was there a light on inside. "It's dead, isn't it?"

"It is, yes."

"I suspected. One of the elements likely used in the compound that carried out has been stolen from the very fridge of our killer's victim. In these ten-year-old '27 models, they used methyl formate. It's highly combustible. But I doubt that this house was exclusively attacked just to steal that—not when there are larger sources of it in the area."

"Well, we already know that! A thief wouldn't commit such a murder as this!" Anthony recognized the voice, and saw that the young officer was getting cocky. He didn't feel inclined to intervene with this cockiness, as he'd be gone from here soon enough. He knew at once that the answer wasn't up to even his great memory for now—they would have to go one of his several libraries to follow what clues he was developing. But like he had previously considered, it was always to be a brief visit.

"I'll check back soon—very soon—with the specifics," Anthony promised the police chief.

"And he really means it!" Tom added. He was about to say something else, when suddenly, the air split with an angry shriek. Jim and Tom, and many of the cops, turned. There was a gap in the ranks of onlookers who had squeezed into the kitchen: two of the officers, and the woman with the camera, had gone missing!

"Someone just grabbed the photographer!" one of the officers yelled. "But we're on him, Mr. Anthony..."

Jim had no reason to disagree with them, but also, nothing was stopping him from joining the two officers in their pursuit. "Hey, Jim!" Tom Gentry yelled suddenly. There was a flush to his face that almost made his freckles vanish. "I can't quite keep up with this—"

The officers in question had stopped at the end of the hallway that had led out of the kitchen. They were still running, but beside Anthony's great speed it was as though they were standing still. Anthony was already preparing to round the corner, when he started envisioning the shape of a javelin in his mind. And he became that javelin as he lunged out. His arms broke a grip held between the escaping man and the photographer—but *she* was the one grabbing *him*. She'd managed to rip herself from the man and was pushing him back, but Anthony saw that too late. Now he was letting the kidnaper escape the kidnapee!

But by making the dive the way he did—and as he twisted from his realization—he landed prone, and by the time he got back up, the man was already in the distance.

The photographer was busy collecting herself, and did so very quickly. "I almost had him," she said to Anthony. Her voice seemed genuinely bitter—but with a nice purr to it.

"I don't know why the man behind this would return to the scene of the crime in the middle of a police investigation."

"Maybe he's just daring...and drawn to something he wanted."

"Something...that wasn't here before?"

Slowly, he realized he had been staring at the ground—and just as slowly, he looked up at the woman.

"My name is Anne Somerset," she said. "My mother was Theodore Sherman's younger sister."

"Isn't there something in police protocol that says that people aren't supposed to be assigned to cases where their relatives are the victims?"

"Also...hold on..." Tom was catching up to the two of them, but had heard what they were saying. "I thought that Sherman didn't have any surviving relatives."

"My mother and uncle are—were—estranged. It *was* a significant age gap."

Anthony flinched at something in her words—something his sixth sense was pointing him towards. "You use the past tense, of course, because your uncle is dead. But I also feel like it's apt to describe your mother...am I right?"

"Yes...I...she went missing two nights ago. I filed a police report as soon as I got into work the next day—but they need more time before they can open a missing persons case."

Anthony let his face relax somewhat, and again, a rare grin appeared. *Something*—and even he didn't entirely know what yet—had entered his mind. He gestured for Tom to head back to the car. "Miss Somerset, would you like to come to the Pueblo with me?"

• • •

The Pueblo, in the Mojave, was where Jim Anthony could breathe again. Free from interruptions from the outside world, it was always staffed by many workers ready to help him for whatever he needed. It was also where he was currently storing some books that he planned to have moved to the Teepee—his other retreat, an enormous mansion in the Catskills. Tom considered that last fact significantly while he listened in on Anthony and Miss Somerset talking in the back of the plane. Jim was asking her more about her mother. To Tom, it was obvious that Jim saw some reason to be suspicious of the elder woman, as if the estrangement was not merely a matter of age, and that there could be some sort of revenge planned. But Anthony did a good job of disguising his words, while doing his best to be truly honest to the young lady. He didn't suspect her directly, after all. And Anne seemed to be telling the truth—that she really knew absolutely nothing about her uncle, aside from his public image.

As Jim slowly ran out of questions to ask her, he kept the conversation alive. Tom decided to cut out at this point. He didn't want to lean in on Jim's charisma. He didn't know if Jim had his eye on the girl in more ways than one, but if he did, he figured it would be best to let nature run its course.

Evidently the conversation was still good! As Tom landed the plane, they came out still talking about a specific rare variant of flower that Anthony had written some footnotes on. "The girl's a gardener," Tom said with a shrug, to none but his. He stifled a laugh at seeing Jim Anthony with red cheeks, which didn't fade at all as the two talked. Many years had he traveled with him, and yet rarely had he seen crimson come to the detective's bronze flesh!

He was in the process of leading the photographer into where he kept his unequaled collection of research materials. As he led her through several of its intricate hallways, he arrived at the library. As they arrived, however, Jim froze, and footsteps approached. Tom, leading behind, could quietly tell Jim was judging the girl's reaction to hearing footsteps. She kept her cool as a figure creeped towards them—she had good reason too, after all, for this was a shriveled old man. Of the frail variety, that is to say, not the sort that has the tendency to defy age to prey upon beautiful women.

"You didn't ring the gongs when you landed," the figure whispered, with a hint of warmth in his voice.

"It's good to see you again, Grandfather," Anthony said to Mephito. "This is Miss Somerset. She and I were in a conversation that I didn't want to put on pause while I came here to look at a particular piece of the book collection."

"It's nice to meet you, friend of James Anthony," Mephito said, shaking

Anne's hand. "Is there a book you'd like in particular, my son?"

"I actually know right where it is. One second, I'll get it."

And suddenly, the detective bounded forward, with his calf muscles visibly tightened, exposed as they were from the shorts he was wearing. Even through his casual sweatshirt, one could see the chords of his back. Catching himself on his hands, he flipped himself outward and bounded again, lunging high onto the bookshelf he'd indicated, and taking a tome from it—then, holding himself up by only one hand, he spun around and dived back towards the other three.

"Not quite going for humility today, is he?" Mephito said to himself with awe.

"It...ought to pass soon," Tom replied, half-jokingly. Anthony didn't seem to hear them, and opened the book. Already, however, both Anthony's pilot and grandfather were noticing (having been trained in this by the diligence of Jim himself) that the detective was positioning himself very particularly before Anne.

Almost casually, the Irish-Indian sleuth murmured, "Ah, yes, that's the story—Greek fire!"

And very quickly, his nearly-black eyes snapped up to meet those of the photographer. Tom couldn't see her face from this angle, and just as quickly Jim closed the book.

"I can give you my card, Miss Somerset—perhaps we can arrange some time to talk about those, uh... 'mutual sciences,' as you called them. I think I'll have one of the staff fly you home, if that's alright."

"Of course—"

And Tom interrupted. "I could take her back, if you want, Jim..." But again the dark eyes flashed.

"I wanted to consult you about something in private, Tom," Jim said—*very* casually.

Tom kept control over his face. "As you say, boss."

"I can escort Miss Somerset out—perhaps in that time, I can make up for any lost hospitality," Mephito said helpfully. He set his gentle hands on her shoulders, and began to lead her away. When he was sure she wasn't looking, the old man glanced over his own shoulder and winked at Jim.

Jim waited a few moments, when he was sure his grandfather and the photographer had gone.

"Go let the flight crew for the *Thunderbird* know that one of our special beacons has to be put on one of Miss Somerset's effects." The *Thunderbird* was Jim's private plane—one of the most sophisticated ever built. "I assume Grandfather has managed to let them know that they needed to get one ready. I sent him a Morse code signature through a hidden transmitter to be at the Pueblo, rather than the Teepee, and to be ready."

Tom was taken aback. "But...why, Jim?"

"The Pueblo was meant to be set up to trap whoever I brought back to it, since after all we couldn't take her to the Teepee—that place is even more important, and can only be reached by parachute, as you know. I figured one of the people who would arrive at the crime scene would be linked to the crime itself. Or at least, that was one eventuality I was prepared for. And fortunately, it paid off!"

"You mean this has all been to trap...to trap Miss Somerset? To put a spy-device on her?" Tom asked.

"Yes. Remember, she has a personal stake in her uncle's murder. She may be the murderer herself—or her mother is the murderer. In any case—I do believe she's close to who's responsible. The one the cops said called him- or herself 'the Flame Wizard.'"

"And all this just...came to you?" Tom exclaimed. But then he remembered what abilities his friend possessed—and also that he had been *testing* the photographer, with his various glances. He was gauging her reactions to key bits of information. "That sixth sense can present some real riddles sometimes." And he remembered the task Anthony had set him to. "I'll go alert the staff! You tell me the rest when I'm back!"

· · ·

Eventually Anne—and her bugged shoe, which had both a radar tracking tag and a tiny microphone and transmitter—were on their way back to New York City. Mephito and Tom returned to the library, where Jim was already on his way to the garage. He beckoned them to follow. "The Flame Wizard deserves his name," he was saying. "He stumbled upon the secret of Greek fire. It was a weapon the Byzantines used against their enemies. Alchemists sought its formula throughout the Middle Ages—and even modern chemical discoveries have only let us ape the mythical image, with the flamethrower used during the Great War."

"It sounds like a terrible weapon for a man of little sense to have," Mephito said grimly.

"Agreed. I suspect we'll never truly know what Greek fire is, but whoever the Flame Wizard happens to be, he has a reasonable proxy of it. An active ingredient is methyl formate, and even I'd be hard-pressed to synthesize the rest to do exactly what I thought it did—that displacement of thermal energy."

"I remember," Tom said, and Jim gave him a little time to inform his grandfather about what had taken place, in regards to the nature of the murder.

"We'll need motive, though, so we're going to follow Anne based on the idea that she's associated with the killer. Grandfather—I also used the signal to let the garage know we'd be needing these miniature trucks."

"I hope they grant you great speed in your search, my son," Mephito replied. "You will need to work quickly, before anyone in the City notices that you have returned. It must seem like you were drawn on a false quest to another part of the country. I'll wait here should the Pueblo be needed again."

"The police force will deny that I'm there if it comes up, too," Jim said. "I'll see you again soon, Wise One. I'm sorry that my visits are always so brief!"

"I'm just grateful to have a descendant who carries such great responsibility. You know I'll always be waiting. May the spirits of the Comanche be with you, as always."

"And with you, Grandfather."

Thus Mephito remained behind as Jim led Tom out to the truck. "We'll take shifts driving," Jim said then, playfully. "It's a long way back to New York."

• • •

When it wasn't Anthony's turn at the wheel, he got a radio confirmation from the NYPD. "The City still believes you're pursuing your research, Jim," the chief had said. Jim explained in turn that as a matter of safety, he couldn't give even the police too many details. As he and Tom knew (while the cops didn't), the enemy may come from within—from the coroner's office, to be precise. What was more, by a very deliberate hand—Anthony had, through Anne, perchance informed the Flame Wizard that he was aware of the use of Greek fire in the death of Theodore Sherman. There would have to be a meeting in which she passed on this information, of course, and Jim Anthony would be outside that meeting, listening in! And if Anne was the killer herself, perhaps a remark made in private would reveal her guilt.

What followed next, Tom realized, was a stakeout. It was a mobile one, to stay in range of the microphone—they didn't specifically follow Anne, and Tom saw this was Jim trying to believe in her innocence. Yet after several days of camping out—plus those spent on the road from the Mojave—they were both delighted to finally strike paydirt. "Miss...Somerset..." a voice came over the radio. It was distorted by Anne's walking, and thus came out scratchy and with many words cut out. "So...of you...join us."

After a second of apprehension, the sound of Anne's shoes hitting the floor stopped, and Anthony and Tom heard some sounds that indicated she had sat down. "Where is she, Tom?" Jim Anthony asked.

"Pascallini's, the Italian restaurant on Fifth!" Tom cried. "I'm on it!"

Jim couldn't help but tense up as the car jerked forward, though not through any fault in Tom's driving—it was because to him, this was the greatest excitement. Service to the public was what he always aimed for, whether he was in the laboratory or here, in the car, rocketing towards any chance to stop a great evil. His grandfather's words echoed in his mind. The Flame Wizard clearly had the power to do whatever he (or she) wanted, and though she or he had had his revenge on Theodore Sherman, there was the chance that this meeting indicated that the Wizard's activities weren't yet over. In any case, for the sake of justice for crimes both present and future, the fight had to end then and there.

Indeed, it was exciting to improve the world from a laboratory. But for Jim Anthony, he was needed the most on the battlefield. Even if, in addition to science and—all this—he also sometimes was a philosopher. The sweat-lodge at the Pueblo had facilitated such an impulse. And now, his philosophical experiences were making him ask the question...

When would his quest be over? When would there be a day that evil stopped?

However, he was often capable of bifurcating his mind, and half of his thoughts were focused on the sounds coming over the radio from the bug. "Now...business," the voice was saying. Was it the voice of the Flame Wizard, or merely a servant? Regardless, the voice was male, unless the speaker was very good at disguising her voice. "You have...formation on the pro...of Jim Anthony?"

"Yes, damn you." This voice was much clearer—it was Anne! "He knows you're using the...fire."

"Very clever of him." Both voices were getting clearer as they got ever nearer to Pascallini's. "Good measure of his intellect, of course. But he knows nothing of the holdings in Guatemala?"

"No. No, he'd have no way of knowing—even for a man of his ability, that couldn't happen so early in the case."

"Very well." But there was an odd pause just as Tom put the car in park outside the Italian restaurant. "That car, there—isn't that...?" And suddenly, Jim's blood ran cold.

How had they recognized the...? This was no time for words—only actions, now. Anthony almost tore the door off scrambling out of the car. He bolted for the door of the restaurant, but he could see from one of the window seats that a man, sitting at the same table as Anne, was making a break for it! Even Jim's eyes, though, couldn't track the man's face and follow him at the same time. As he broke into the restaurant Anne rose to stop him.

"He escaped through the kitchen, Jim!" Anne was saying. "He may be trying the same trick he used on my uncle!"

Anthony was in the kitchen in seconds—no time to find his target. "Everyone!!" he cried. "Get out now—there's a bomb!"

On cue came the screaming. Jim Anthony was back at the door again before any time had passed, making sure the patrons and staff alike could get out into the streets. He checked and double-checked that Anne in particular was away from the building.

He was in the process of removing the last chef, when as expected, there was a terrible flash of light from the back of the restaurant. A churning pyre had broken out—even the mere residual heat in the kitchen had been enough to trigger the effect of the sinister element!

Anthony knew there'd be no time for the fire department to arrive before the building was lost. Sprinting back down to the car, he saw that Tom was already emerging. "Holy Gee-man-ee, it's Chicago Part Two!"

"Or London, 1666. Quick, Tom, the emergency hose!"

There was a fire hydrant right outside the restaurant—its sole salvation. While Tom searched the truck for the hose, Jim knelt besides the bright red contraption and emptied his mind, his eyes slowly closing. What he was about to do required skills considered advanced even by his standards. He would always have a deep respect for the masters, of Asia and of his own tribe (as well as many other bands throughout the country, such as the Plains Cree people), who had taught him the hidden strengths of what his Western kinsmen from the Irish side of his family perhaps oversimplified under the name "martial arts." (He was almost completely sure his father, Shean Boru Anthony, from whom the Irish blood had come, had shared his respect of these styles in his own almost-inevitable mutual study of them.) Many of these diverse disciplines had a common tenet, which Jim Anthony was tapping into at this very moment: through concentration, any feat is possible.

In a way that seemed to be without warning, his eyes snapped back open, and with the sound of a thick branch whipping through the air, the side of his hand slammed against the fire hydrant. Even the hard steel shattered against Anthony's blow. The highly pressurized water burst out, and without any heed, Tom cried out, "Jim!" and tossed the hose to the tall dark detective. Anthony quickly fitted the hose around the rushing water—again his legendary concentration returned, bolstered once more by strength that bordered on impossible. The hulking pilot was at Anthony's side in an instant, holding the hose in place as Jim unleashed its power on the flames in the kitchen.

The smoke was blinding, and flashing heat of the flames hurt Jim's tough skin. These flames lasted while the ones at Sherman's estate had gone away before spreading. But perhaps the perpetrator had used a great quantity of the Greek fire, and great quantities of the compound were enough to ignite such a mighty blaze. He also became aware of trickling water around his feet—presumably the remains of the ice that had formed after the chemical had gone off.

In time, the two men were able to stop the fire. The building still wasn't safe, and was severely damaged, but it could reopen soon.

Both men were exhausted, but they didn't even get a chance to fully exit the building before Anne Somerset was back inside. "Anne, stay back," Jim said. "It's not entirely safe..." But suddenly, he found the beautiful redhead was already making a point of standing *very* much within his personal space.

"I wanted to make sure *you* were safe," she replied, in a low, husky voice. The bitterness she'd displayed when first she spoke to him was replaced completely with an attractive, compassionate honesty. At least, so it sounded to Tom. They still had reason to be suspicious of her.

"How—how did you find me here?" she asked then.

"We put a bug on your shoe," Jim replied. He was trembling somewhat—only his training keeping him from revealing more.

At once the photographer's face dropped with disappointment. "I take it you don't trust me, then."

"We had our reasons," Jim said, quietly hoping it would be an adequate explanation.

"After our talk, I'd become fond of you, Jim. How could you think I was *voluntarily* in league with the man who killed my uncle?"

"You *were* having a conversation with the Flame Wizard, or an associate of his."

"The Flame Wizard is threatening me!" she cried. "He approached me two days ago, and said he'd give me a chance he never gave my uncle. I could work with him, or he would murder me, to complete his revenge! He said conscripting me was enough for replacement vengeance—but if I slipped up in giving him the scoop on you, he'd take the full penalty! I don't even know how he found out you took me to that base of yours, Jim. I swear it!"

Tom Gentry waited to see if the photographer could melt the heart of Jim Anthony. And sure enough—she did. After a few moments, his face seemed to relax.

"Alright, Anne. I'm sorry. But it's good we came here nonetheless. If you give me your shoe, I'll remove the bug." After he did so, he said, "Who was the man you were meeting with? A lieutenant of the one we're hunting?"

"No—that *was* the Flame Wizard."

"He was? Good Lord, Anne, what's his identity?"

"I don't know. I didn't recognize his face. He can't be a famous person."

Anthony was silent for some time. "Let's get out of here, you two," he said at last. And they returned to the truck. At Anthony's request, Tom started driving towards the airport, where the *Thunderbird* was waiting.

• • •

"So, Miss Somerset, I'm sure Jim is meaning to ask you," the Irish pilot began, once they were all aboard the plane. They were all in the cockpit and he was searching for the guides the bird carried for Central America. "What did the Wizard mean about them 'holdings in Guatemala'?"

"He didn't exactly go into detail about them," Anne replied, with that bitterness again—though not directed at Tom, of course. "But during an earlier phone conversation he mentioned a word. It sounded foreign— Pete's Caw?"

Jim closed his eyes for a second, lost in thought. "Once you find the atlas for Guatemala, Tom, give it here. I think I remember something from a story my mother told me, when my father was away on one of his journeys. It was the story of an adventure he had south of Mexico..."

When Tom gave him the guidebook in question, he paged through the index of town names. Updated by Jim's father, via notes he took on his many quests into the unknown, it logged villages that were ignored or not

"I take you don't trust me then."

familiar to many cartographers. Rarely did Jim have to use these note-books, but now they would definitely be quite handy.

"Here we are: Peets'kaah. An old Mayan village, due east of Suchiate in the state of Chiapas—that's got to be it."

"Where's the closest airport, is the real question?" Tom asked then.

Jim grinned. "That's where we're in luck, old friend," he said. "According to my father's charts, there's a large valley just a few miles from Peets'kaah. It could land the *Thunderbird*. I trust your skill."

"Well, thank you, Jim. Say—I don't suppose we could run into that lady fighter friend of yours who hangs out down South—Flores is her name, isn't it?"

"Ah, yes, Maria. I think she and her girls are taking care of some other business for now. But maybe we'll see them again soon."

Jim found himself smiling. His female operators were among the most efficient. It *was* too bad that Maria Flores often found herself taking care of some battle or another.

"It's going to be a long flight, friends," Tom Gentry said eventually. "I've got my coffee, Jim. You and Anne can go back and get some rest."

"I won't need any," Jim said. What he said was the truth, for two rea-sons: one, Jim Anthony could go without sleep for many days past the normal expiration date for many men; and two, when faced with a serious problem like this, Jim Anthony *couldn't* sleep from excitement; so intense was his thinking. But suddenly, Anne Somerset was at his arm.

"I'd like to keep chatting with you," she said. "I hope you don't mind, Tom?"

Tom thought he caught her line of thinking, but realized that maybe he was projecting. Nonetheless, the possible reference made him feel awk-ward. He knew that Jim *was* strong lady-bait, after all, and while some men like Jim were genuinely not interested in that sort of thing for one reason or another, Jim was not one of those men in such a way. He didn't know to what level it was good for him to know these things.

"Er, of course not, Miss Somerset," he said. "I hope you two have stellar... communication."

Jim realized Anne had taken his hand and therefore couldn't resist as she left the cockpit.

"Well, then, uh...what did you want to discuss, Anne?" Jim said as he settled.

"Last time, you'll remember we were talking about flowers," she replied.

"Yes?"

"I wanted to hear if you knew of any more of the really *exotic* ones."

"Like...what? I've never found evidence of man-eating flowers, or talking ones, if that's what you're asking."

"You kidder! No, I mean—have you ever heard of, say, *Antirrhinum imperius*?"

Jim blinked.

"No."

"Well, you must be familiar with *something* that most people aren't familiar with?"

"Hm." There was a pause. "There is *Rosa fragor*," he mused.

For a second, Anne seemed nervous, but Jim looked at the space above her shoulder. Her face became a smile, in time. "Interesting genus to bring up."

"Roses?"

"Yeah." She scooted closer to him, and he felt his face darken. "Roses are very romantic to most people, you know. A symbol of Venus—of...well, affection."

Jim was suddenly silent, but if he had tried to speak, he would have been silenced anyway. The red lips were upon his in an instant. Anne Somerset didn't waste her time, especially on a man like Jim Anthony.

Slowly, he decided to embrace her.

And it turned out something *would* knock out Jim Anthony for the evening.

• • •

The two awoke together when Tom yelled from the cockpit that they were landing in Guatemala. Jim had induced a lucid dream to continue to work on the problem as he slept. Anne, however, had had a dreamless but nonetheless restful sleep, and so she woke and stretched smiling. They both got dressed and went out into the main cabin, where Tom was already getting ready to disembark them.

"You look like you're about to faint, old friend," Jim Anthony said then.

"No, Jim, it's alright—I mean, I'll have to sleep soon, but I'll be okay."

Jim merely nodded. He knew of Tom's toughness—it had served him well before in aiding him.

The trio stepped out of the plane into the moist jungle air. It had been some time since Jim had been south of the United States. The humidity was a nice contrast to the cool air of the Teepee, and the dryness of the

Pueblo. Yet he wasn't here on vacation. He could come back here later, per-haps in the name of research, which would relax him. For now he started sprinting into the jungle, suddenly ignorant to the presence of both Anne and Tom.

This would turn out to be a rare mistake on behalf of Jim Anthony.

Soon he was upon the village of Peets'kaah. Already his hawk-like eyes were taking in a strange sight—it was day, and yet no one was outside. His sixth sense was triggered at once, and he saw his mistake of leaving Tom behind.

That was when all the doors of the village burst open—they were mod-ern enough houses—and men in military uniforms burst out. They were armed with similarly-modern machine guns. Jim turned cold as he saw them, and they began firing at him before he could react.

Well—almost!

Immediately, he was able to snap into a diving kick. The bullets had been tellingly aimed at his head, and therefore he was below their paths. As he slid across the jungle mud, he pulled himself forward, and, as he had in the library, used his hands to propel himself. He knocked one guard down, and was back on his feet in time to knock down two more with a kick. "Shoot him!" one of them shouted. *"Kill Jim Anthony!"*

He bounded to the remaining ones at the outer edge, though he was still flanked on the side by two. His great fists and flexible kicks slammed out his first targeted foe—it was a combination of his previously used martial arts, and a simple, improvised style that he felt was appropriately American. The underdog tactic of the one-two punch.

He turned to face the only two conscious soldiers. One of them, having lost his gun, removed his helmet (one of the ones used by soldiers in the Great War, Jim mused) and hurled it at the detective. He ducked out of the way and seized a fallen rifle. But he didn't fire—he returned the throw, and the heavy gun knocked the wind out of the attacker. The other man fired at Anthony but was out of bullets. He'd shot them all in the middle of the fray, missing everything but the open sky. But he had a knife in his hand in an instant, and he was about to jerk Anthony forward, to introduce his abdomen to the blade!

As the man rushed forward, the detective grabbed his arm and changed the direction of his lunge downward. The soldier flipped over his shoulder and blacked out when he hit the ground. The knife didn't get anywhere near his belly.

Jim couldn't waste any time. The village was a trap, and though it had been a quick fight (given the odds), Tom and Anne should have been behind him. He ran back into the jungle, knowing that if he was wrong and there were more clues in the village, he could always return.

But sure enough, as he returned to the valley, Anne was holding a gun up to Tom Gentry's head on the boarding ramp to the *Thunderbird*.

"Where did you and the Flame Wizard put the villagers, Anne?" was Jim's first question.

"They're safe—we coerced them to move to a nearby town and to keep their mouths shut. With the aid of the soldiers, of course. Those soldiers were given a drug that will cause them to obey the Wizard even without pay! You were supposed to die, of course, but the drug must have made the guards sluggish! No matter. You won't stop me from forcing Tom to take me back to Crete. No one can help you in time! You're too far from any of your bases!"

Jim Anthony said nothing, and let her lead Tom back into the plane. However, as they stared at each other through the glass of the cockpit, Anthony mouthed to Tom that he would find them.

Anne had given an inadequate explanation for all of this, but she had reversed Anthony's trick upon him efficiently enough. The Flame Wizard was clearly a lunatic, evidenced if anything by his meticulous paranoia. Not only had Anne suspected or known that the Pueblo trip was meant to expose a possible connection between her and her uncle's murderer, but the conversation between her and the Wizard had been faked. They had probably arranged to have those fake conversations every so often in case Anthony or any another upholder of the law was listening in on them. He entertained the possibility that Anne was a sociopath, and that was how she was able to act so convincingly. But it was entirely possible she was driven by a much more common madness—a madness for power, either through violence and threats, or through economic conquest via her uncle's inheritance.

And yet, the fortune was in control of the board of Sherman Financial. Theodore Sherman had been ignorant of his heirs by blood. The Wizard likely knew that Anne wouldn't see a cent, and this opened Jim's mind to the possibility that the board members could be the next targets.

All the same, determining the cause of villainy was becoming muddled even in the mind of Jim Anthony. By this point so many men and women crazed by greed, illness, or bad luck had crossed his path—and left so many scars on the history of the world. Human beings always seemed to find a way to be evil. He openly admitted to himself that he *hated* it, and yet the hate was tempting him. It made him weak. But in any case, considering the problem of evil, and his own feelings about it, wouldn't get him any closer to the Flame Wizard—and Tom.

. . .

The tussle in the village had rubbed mud all over Jim's shirt, but more significantly, it had torn it. In this line of work, clothes didn't last very long. As he dashed through the jungle he tore off the remaining scraps of his shirt and removed his khaki shorts, leaving him in his trademark yellow bathing trunks. No human eyes were here to admire his musculature, which pressed tight against the tough bronzed skin. It took several miles of running before the skin began to glisten with sweat.

He swept his eyes around wildly as he ran, making sure that no snakes hung from the branches overhead, and that he did not step on or run into any poisonous spiders. All the while, he was hoping to find the "nearby village" that the inhabitants of Peets'kaah had seemingly been relocated to before it got too dark. More predators would be out then.

But Jim had the Anthony luck, and there was one of the feared animals out in the day. There she stalked, her spots clear in the afternoon sun— a huge jaguar. She had her eyes on Jim. He wondered maybe if he was close to her young. Such a thing would be certain to provoke an attack! Or, maybe, she was simply hungry—but he didn't want to chance on her *not* being a man-eater!

And sure enough, perhaps again with help by the Anthony luck, she lunged. He tried to catch her slender form and sling her away over his head, but he hadn't counted on those wicked claws. Even the seasoned Jim Anthony cried out in pain as the cat's claws cut into his flesh. The slices weren't too long but they were deep. The pain gave him desperation, and it was this that enabled him to throw the cat away. She gave a shriek of pain as he did.

He wanted to preserve this beautiful creature as best as he could. Specimens like her were valuable to the natural world.

So far, however, he had succeeded in enraging the beast. She was on her feet again, and prepared to charge him. He glanced upward, seeing a tree branch low enough for him to make—*if* he strained himself. He'd have only one chance. Another blow from the jaguar's body would knock him off his feet, and she could pin him. Then it was only a matter of removing his heart from his chest with those claws.

He squatted briefly, and tensed the necessary muscles. Swiftly, he bounded off the ground, narrowly evading the big cat's jump. His strong hands seized the thick branch, and with a short grunt he pulled himself into the tree. Down below, the cat snarled at him, slashing at the tree's trunk futilely. Jim Anthony couldn't help but grin. "Maybe next time, old girl."

He turned to look for other branches that could support his weight. He'd travel like this, jumping from tree to tree, until he'd significantly outpaced the jaguar. After he started this sort of travel, however, he kicked himself—metaphorically of course. To the village, all he had to do was climb to the top of the trees and see over the rest of the jungle!

It was when he seized a higher branch that something up above caught his eye. It appeared at first as if the vines above had become horribly animated by some unknown intelligence. But in truth, the moving things about weren't vines—they were an enormous *python*, which was slithering down to begin wrapping itself around Anthony's sturdy form!

These snakes couldn't eat human beings—their jaws couldn't stretch that far—but the creature didn't know that, and was content to constrict the detective to death. Even as the scaly coils curled around Anthony's body, he seized it while desperately trying not to lose his grip on the tree. It was heavy, being the largest living specimen he had seen before in person. It was hard not to be afraid of what it could do even a big man.

But he ripped it away from himself, doing his best not to permanently harm it. He had to yank it off the tree in order to truly get it away from him. As he dropped it down, he hoped the fall wouldn't hurt it—it was merely following its nature, after all, just as the jaguar had; just as it was Jim's nature to avoid the perils in his path to get after Tom.

He *would* have to return here for a vacation, if things got too dull. The beasts of the jungle were among the very few who could present a physical challenge to him—and uncovering the secrets of the forest would be a good test of his brain.

As he escaped the horizon of the trees, the Anthony luck often shined bright as much as it had a tendency to complicate things, especially when he followed the impulses of his nature. In the distance he could spot a clearly populated town.

• • •

As Jim Anthony entered the Guatemalan village, he passed through a shopping district, where he heard a gasp passing one of the stalls. He wondered at first if it was related to his naked torso, which displayed the jaguar's claw marks. (Presently he was trying to take humor from the awkward situation). Turning towards the gasp, he saw that the stall in question appeared to sell antiques from both Mayan and colonial times. The woman running it was so tiny that she almost seemed to come from the same time as some of her wares; not even ancient Mephito was so withered. But as she stared as Anthony, she had an animation in her eyes that seemed very youthful.

"Anthony, you've—come back!" she whispered in accented English. "You're still so—young!"

But Jim smiled. "My name is James Anthony. I believe that you must have met my father, Shean Anthony. You can call me Jim, though. How did you make the acquaintance of my father?"

"Oh, more than acquaintance, young man. He and I were truly great friends! We met when I was trying to get myself on my feet in Guatemala City, after losing a past establishment—the one I'd been running for most of my life! He taught me English, so I could work with businessmen from the United States if I had to, and bought me a sizable collection of pieces to sell. You'll notice I've stayed humble, but thanks to your father's generosity I'm never in need." She paused. "My name is Isabella, by the way."

"Nice to meet you, Isabella. My father's newspaper, the *New York Star*, is in my hands now, as is his fortune. Should your town or any of its neighbors ever be in need, please don't hesitate to contact me through their office."

"You've inherited Shean's greatest gift of all, Jim Anthony—his enormous heart."

Jim smiled proudly in memory of his father. But his face reflected thoughtfulness as he had a brief debate with himself about the limits of luck.

"I don't suppose you happen to have any antique books in your wares?"

"I do, as a matter of fact. You wouldn't find them terribly interesting, I think—field guides to plants is what they are. Mighty old, of course..."

Jim Anthony blessed the circumstances that so often appeared in his extraordinary life.

"I've been running into some recurring references to flowers, recently. I'd be happy to buy some of the older guides."

At first, the old woman protested Anthony actually paying for the books, but upon seeing how *truly* old they were, Jim insisted on being fair. He was giving her trouble by paying in U.S. dollars, anyway, he explained. Once he had the books he examined it. Under the *Antirrhinum* (or snapdragon) section, he found a reference that no longer appeared in modern field guides, due to the species' extinction: *Antirrhinum imperius.* Imperius meant "control" in Latin. The nectar of the "control snapdragon" did exactly what the name implied: it made the human mind highly suggestible. That had been both foreshadowing and a taunt from Anne: the Flame Wizard had the snapdragon's nectar, or a facsimile thereof, and had managed to create soldiers from it...

And then there was the plant whose name she had called from his subconscious, by speaking so often of flowers. *Rosa fragor.* It was an exceptionally rare rose, whose stems contained a toxic sap. Anthony had studied this sap before and remembered its unique chemical structure. He wondered what would happen if such a chemical was combined with methyl formate.

He had no paper to write on, and he didn't want to damage the book, so he took a handkerchief from his trunks and produced a pen from his pocket. Kneeling at the stall, he began to jot down various chemical formulae in an attempt to discern the effects the chemical would have in heat above room temperature.

After about twenty minutes, he had solved it. His brain had been sorting the problem slowly and Anne's taunt had caused him to realize that *Rosa fragor* and methyl formate were the secret to Greek fire. But he hadn't *overtly* seen it until now.

"Isabella, you've been of invaluable aid," he said. "I need to get to Europe—to the island of Crete in the Mediterranean."

"You think I would take your American money if I didn't have a way to get to the bank in Guatemala City? It's a three hour ride, but I manage. There's an airport there, of course."

"Excellent! If you're fine with transporting me, it would be a great boon."

"Of course. Why don't you rest at my house? It's over there—nothing is ever too far away here."

She pointed to a humble place diagonally across the street from her stall. Though it looked small, even for one person, it had a garage and a lawn much like many of the suburbs of the U.S. "If the ride is a few hours," Jim said, "I'm in no position to decline your great hospitality."

"I'll be with you when the sun begins to set," the shopkeeper said with a smile.

Jim took the time not to sleep, but to meditate, sitting cross-legged in the center of an old sofa. He was still rested from what he'd allowed himself on the plane. During this time he double and triple checked his chemical calculations, while largely focusing, somewhat against his will, on Anne.

He accepted the fact that she had beguiled him, even as his training kept him suspicious of her. He could have gotten closer to the Flame Wizard if her obvious intelligence hadn't made him think of certain...possibilities. But he remembered her physical attributes, and knew that he had possibly mistaken lust for a romantic connection. They hadn't known each other for very long, after all.

There was the chance that the Flame Wizard was also using *Antirrhinum imperius* on her, and not just the soldiers. Given that she was acting very independently, however, it was relatively unlikely.

His meditation was broken when Isabella returned home. "I hope you've been comfortable," she said.

"Absolutely," Jim replied with a smile. "Now, I hate to put pressure on you, but it's paramount that we go to the City at once. I didn't want to impose upon your business..."

"And there are few others here who travel as I do—very few, these days. Let us head to the garage, young Anthony."

"Yes! I'm curious to see what model car you drive."

"Car?" Suddenly, the frail old woman burst out in laughter. "Oh, my boy, I do not drive a car."

She took him out to the garage. Standing there, shiny even in the diminished light of the setting sun, was a '36 model Harley-Davidson!

Even Jim Anthony was shaken by seeing Isabella's ride of choice. But he, too, saw the humor in the situation. It was a great relief, when faced with such a serious threat, to see someone who took something that others saw in them as a weakness, who either made it into a strength, or ignored the pain of it. In this case, Isabella's age was her power, not her handicap.

They both mounted the motorcycle, with Jim in the back. Isabella had given a spare helmet, and without a word, she sped out of the garage and cut down the dusty jungle road.

• • •

Three hours later, Jim Anthony was shaking Isabella's tiny hand. "Your bike's speed is really impressive—as are your driving skills in the dark," he was saying. "It's been a true honor."

"Well, to meet the son of Shean Boru Anthony was never an honor I expected," she said. "I hope you catch this evil Wizard."

"I hope so too. I'll see you again, my friend."

She nodded with the smirk of a confident teenager on her face. Then she sped off.

The airport had agreed to let Anthony use one of their smaller planes himself, once the detective proved his identity. Many of the staff had gasped upon comparing the man before them to the photo from the front page headline, which had been declaring Jim Anthony's quest to stop the Flame Wizard. A pilot, Julio, had agreed to fly Anthony to Crete. When Jim saw how much Julio's hands were shaking, and how much sweat covered his scalp, he set his hand on the young man's shoulder. "Relax," he said calmly. "I trust your skill as a pilot."

"I hope I-I can live up to the standard of Tom Gentry, Señor Anthony," the piloted stuttered.

"Neither I nor my assistants are worth such, uh, gravity, Julio. We're human, like the rest of you. I just happen to have been really lucky as far as my inheritances. The rest is hard work...and a lot of sleep loss."

The mustachioed pilot took Anthony at his word, and seemed a lot more laid back when they took off. It was another long flight, but with the detective's advice, the pilot was able to maximize his speed. When they reached Crete it was mid-morning. He would sleep a bit before returning to Guatemala City. He was so drowsy he barely noticed the lengths to which Jim Anthony went to thank him. When Julio had fallen asleep Anthony left him a sizable tip.

The issue was—where in Crete was the Flame Wizard's base? It wasn't exactly a small place.

That was ignoring the chance, too, that the reference to Crete had been a ruse!

But somehow he doubted it. Anne's demeanor was one of smug pride over finally being able to show her true colors. And certain details like the fake kidnapping plot, and the staged trap meetings, showed that the Flame Wizard, too, was showy and arrogant when exposed. Here, in the capital of Heraklion, the Wizard would meet the end to his plots.

When Jim Anthony entered the city limits, even the Christians living in Heraklion had brief intrusive thoughts about Apollo coming back. Indeed Anthony's tanned skin tone—and the fact that he hadn't gotten any new clothes in Guatemala City—made him resemble the legendarily attractive god. If Jim had let himself realize that that was how they thought of him, he would have been uncomfortable. As he had said to Julio—he was just a man. Sometimes he loathed his public persona. There were few places in the world where he could escape adulation or cries for aid. Someday, perhaps, he would meet someone who could help him truly enter the world of mortal men—or there would come a time when someone would eclipse him.

Not wanting to continue on half naked, he located a second hand clothing store and there, with his remaining cash, purchased worn jeans and a new shirt which was a size small. He left the front unbuttoned and rolled up the sleeves as he left the store. He was wondering where to pick up the trail of his prey.

He was not thinking these thoughts long because as he soon as he walked out into the street—the air split with the sound of a gunshot!

The bullet missed him by scant inches, and his eyes scanned ahead swiftly. In a second, he saw the barrel of a sniper rifle—in the hands of another *Antirrhinum imperius* victim, no doubt! He squeezed the trigger, and that in turn was the trigger for Jim Anthony's reflexes. He sprinted forward just as the bullet left the barrel, and it smacked loudly on the cobblestones of the street. Anthony charged for the building the shooter had fired from. The old brownstone's door was dark with rot—it was a terrible headquarters and was likely taken only because the building had been abandoned. Not even a medium shove from his shoulder was necessary to break the door down.

More men in infantry uniforms! More brainwashed slaves, too, in all likelihood. They had the same semi-automatics as all the others Anthony had faced. As they marched towards him, he saw that several more were emerging from a downward staircase. This place had a basement—no doubt the true center of operations!

He dove forward again, his left fist finding a throat, and his right, a stomach. The guards grunted, and he wondered if perhaps his blows could shake them out of their trances. But the snapdragon was potent, and so he had to swing around to take them down—driving blows into the backs of their necks. Then he spun again, to face the soldiers coming up the staircase. All the same, his sixth sense was buzzing so strongly that his worry for Tom Gentry deepened. He didn't have time to stop these guys and the sniper when Tom was still in danger.

He decided instead merely to bound over them—having confidence in the fact that he was simply too fast for any of them to draw a bead. Ricocheting off the wall, he was down the stairs, into the basement.

More guards approached him, and what he saw of the basement in that brief time was too cramped for him to jump over them. But amidst their number was a familiar figure. Still dressed in long red was Anne Somerset. "You're surrounded, Jim Anthony!" she cried out. "Give up."

He didn't have a chance to say anything, or even move, before she dashed up to him. She raised her hand and his eyes locked on the shiny carapaces that were her crimson-painted fingernails. He caught onto what she was doing, but there was nothing that could be done—!

The hand came down, and the nails slashed sharply across Jim Anthony's face. He felt the tiny but fast-creeping pain of the toxin she'd put at the edge of that scarlet nail polish. And then he was lost in the depths of sleep.

• • •

When Jim awoke, he found his arms tied above his head. His feet were tied together at the ankles, and all his restraints were bound to a cold metal slab. He sighed, and the vibrations in the air that was the sound of his exhalation indicated he was in a stuffy space—there was something about the quality of the air, he felt, which indicated he was in a sub-basement. Maybe even a sub-sub-basement. He heard murmuring, and as his vision cleared he saw Tom Gentry in much simpler constraints—the captors went for the simple ropes-around-a-chair approach. He had a white handkerchief gag in his mouth, and he was struggling to escape, to give any sort of help to his friend. Jim did not struggle but his intent to aid Tom was just as strong.

Aside from them, there were two other figures. One of them, of course, was Anne. But the other, a man in a red toga and red cowl, holding the vial full of tiny grey pellets, had never been seen before by Jim. But he knew him—he could only be the Flame Wizard. He had a wicked looking long face, what could be seen of it, but he had a smile that befitted the arrogance Jim took him to have. He approached Jim as he saw him awake, and Anne followed closely behind.

"So, this is the great Jim Anthony," the Flame Wizard declared. "You should have known you wouldn't prevail."

Jim kept a great poker face. "Your accent..." he said then. "It's not just your fire that's Greek, is it? You're from around here?"

"I was born and raised in a small village on Crete," the Wizard confirmed then. "You're a man of science, Jim Anthony! And so you may recognize my face when I give its image to you, after denying you such a thing at the restaurant. I was once a great paragon of a scientist, and only through the betrayal of Theodore Sherman did I fall from grace. It was his sick greed that turned the world against me! I once would have revolutionized chemistry with my discovery. Now I spit on the corpse of the man who took it all away from me, and pray his soul sees more fire...in Hell."

"What are you talking about, Wizard? You seem a little eager to show me your identity."

For a second, the Wizard's smile dropped—but trembling, it returned. He threw his head back in a laugh that showed a madness that could only be created by deep suffering. Impulsively, the Wizard seized the seams of his cowl, and pulled it away from his head. As he dropped it, he revealed himself to be of a Mediterranean complexion, fitting his story. He could have passed for any of the people who had seen his sniper shoot at Anthony. Though he was probably around forty, he looked significantly older—his hair was shock-white, and his eyes were wild with some sort of dementia. Anthony could believe at once that this man was a vengeful killer.

"I see you care more to study my face than to hear my story, or to guess at my identity," the Wizard hissed. "But don't worry—I intend to explain everything anyway. Since you probably have forgotten my greatness like all the rest, I will tell you my name: Dr. Alexander Kallinikos. I was the pride and joy of my Cretan village. Against the odds of poverty, I managed to attain an education in both electronics and chemistry. Being able to invent new machines was a way of attaining recognition, due to my natural talent in it, but chemistry was my true passion. On Crete I learned many of the myths of my ancient ancestors. Among them I heard the stories of Greek fire. I had to recreate it. I realized that if I could, I would be hailed as the greatest chemical hero of the age!

"My first invention was something I believe *you* launched one of your creations from! It was a wheeled remote-control platform with a camera on it. The camera could send images to a receiver by radio waves! Not even the piece of technology I referred to of your invention, the bug you put on Miss Somerset's shoe, could do that! But all the same, I applaud your ability to send a tracking signal and a decent sound broadcast to a radio receiver. We must all start *small* after all." And he gave a mocking chuckle.

"It was one of these drones that I used to spy on your garage. That's how I knew what your trucks looked like, Anthony. I would know if you were spying on me, because I was able to inspect your bug and find out its broadcast range. You would have to be very clever to sneak up on me, Anthony! And you underestimated me, it seems. Or perhaps you're not entirely deserving of your reputation."

"We'll never get anywhere if you continually bury me in condescension, Kallinikos," Jim said patiently.

"You're quite right. But remember, I am the master here! All the same, I will continue: I decided to aid my village with the money I made by marketing my device to some military research groups. Given how stupid the world has proven to be I'll doubt they'll use my prototypes at all, despite what benefits they would give them. With my fortune I bought all the real-estate in my town, and therefore was able to help improve my neighbors' homes at will. I left a small portion of my funds aside to bankroll my dream of Greek fire. I was sure to touch on the discovery so soon after my success with the drone.

"But I couldn't find the secret, and soon I was out of money. But I had an ace in the hole, as you Americans say! I could put property from the village as collateral on a massive loan that I planned to take out from Sherman Financial. They will tell you that *I* was the one to be so kind as to put up my whole town, that I *begged* them to take it so I could take more money—that I was desperate, that I was deranged. But everything that happened to my village was *their* fault—was Anne's uncle's fault. For the small amount I wanted, he laughed as he forced me to sign over every last house, farm, and market. I knew that the discovery of Greek fire was my only hope for obtaining the money I would make would let me pay off the loan, and save my village.

"But the first month was shorter than it seemed, and I had no time to waste on other projects. Nothing else paid the bills in that time, for I was flat broke. I *had* to discover the secret in that time, but I didn't. I pleaded for more time, but, mocking me the whole time, they took my village away.

"I cannot guess what happened to them. Presumably their fate was terrible—their poverty worse than it was before. Theodore Sherman, of course, was responsible. His cruel standards were what prevented me from obtaining the key to my wealth, and he made all my struggles in vain. The worst part of it was that after dodging men I presumed to be agents of Sherman Financial, I made the discovery, as you know! And it was during that time that I learned the power of *Antirrhinum imperius*, while studying *Rosa fragor*. I used it to make an army of slaves who would help me establish an enterprise around the world. All because when it was time for me to kill Theodore Sherman, the great Jim Anthony would stand in my way. Anthony's intelligence, of course, was world famous! I would need to have a very elaborate plan to kill him—to kill you.

"Anne Somerset found me while vacationing in Heraklion! I overheard

"But remember, I am the master here!"

her telling a friend of hers that she hated her uncle, and mentioned him by name. We started talking and she told me that she..."

"That I would do anything to attain my uncle's undeserved riches," Anne interrupted then. Jim saw with horror that in her eyes was the same insanity as the Flame Wizard. "I worked hard all my life, and so did my mother, but we never reached his ivory towers. My mother meant no harm to Uncle Theodore, but I was always envious of him. And envious of *you*, Jim! You didn't earn your wealth, either—you got it from your stinking *father*! I should have been richer than both of you!"

"I was originally just going to let you live, and hope that I left no clues," Kallinikos cut in. "But Anne talked about the unjustly wealthy, and she offhandedly mentioned your riches. I asked her casually if she thought you would stop our operation..."

"...and the answer was obviously yes. I know what happens to people who challenge you, Jim—they go to prison, or wind up dead. But not this time! Now we're going to kill you and your assistant, so that we can claim what's ours from my uncle's company, and have our revenge!"

"Anne, I can't speak for you—I only mourn the fact that you're motivated by greed," Jim cut in. "But Kallinikos! What happened here—all the evil you've done—is your fault!"

The Flame Wizard choked, and his face flashed with rage. "How *dare* you accuse the great Kallinikos, the inventor of Greek fire, of...of..."

"Alexander, stop. Greek fire is legendary, yes. Its true identity is elusive, yes! But it was never going to be the greatest scientific discovery in the history of the world. *Weapons* never will be, and industry would have no use for it with today's technology! You let yourself become obsessed with a myth, and the desire to make that myth tangible led you to mortgaging the homes of the people you claimed to love!

"I can assure you that nothing bad happened to your village—ownership of the houses and businesses will likely be restored to the inhabitants, because there's nothing Sherman Financial *could* gain—and your loan will be forgiven anyway, when you get life in jail or a hanging."

Kallinikos let out a cry that sounded like a dying wolf, somehow intelligent and hateful enough to curse its killers with its last breath. But suddenly, the rage melted away into depression. He began to violently sob as he was forced to recognize what he knew all along—it *was* his fault, and he had committed an irreversible crime.

But Anne Somerset was unshaken. She still wanted her revenge on the man whose death she had a hand in, by taking his fortune. She would not let Kallinikos' weakness be her own.

"Snap out of it, you idiot!" she yelled at the Wizard. "We can kill Jim Anthony on a whim as long as he's trapped. Then no one will be able to stop us!"

"But I've failed my people," Kallinikos sobbed. "And my entire life has been a waste. I have no further goals or hopes. He is right about my Greek fire—it is little more than a badge of *shame* for me now!"

As the two argued, Jim's eyes saw that the lab was connected to an elevator shaft. The elevator car waited within. However, across from the shaft was a room with a glass sliding door. Through the glass, he could see large cubes made of the tiny grey pellets of Greek fire. He also realized that as Anne yelled at Kallinikos, the latter was edging towards the door to this storage space. The closer he got, the stronger Jim's sixth sense blazed.

He began to pull both his wrists and ankles apart, feeling for weak points in the coarse fibers. He could snap the ropes soon provided the Flame Wizard made no sudden moves to where he was storing his creation. Slowly, the knots began to break. Tom stared at him and remained silent, even if the flavor of gag was really getting to him.

"You can still be recognized as a scientific genius! I can give you whatever you need, if you help me kill the rest of the company's board and get my uncle's fortune!" Anne shouted.

"There's no point," Kallinikos bemoaned. And he took a significantly large step towards the storeroom. "*There's no point!*" And suddenly, he bolted behind the door.

"Kallinikos, *no!*" Jim yelled. Adrenaline rippled through his body and gave him the second wind he needed. Soon he was away from the plate they'd tied him to, and he ripped the ropes and gag away from Tom Gentry. As he helped Tom up, Jim heard Kallinikos from behind the glass door—which he'd locked. If he was planning to detonate the Greek fire, he'd just turned the storeroom—and maybe even his entire complex—into a tomb!

"I turned off the fan keeping the Greek fire at a safe temperature," the former Flame Wizard said, his voice breaking and straining. "Soon it will reach the...the vital heat. Then there will be nothing of all of us! This whole affair will just be a mystery in time, and that will be the final, *true* legacy of Alexander Kallinikos!"

"Out of my way, you morons!" Anne Somerset screamed then. For the first time in their brief acquaintance, Jim Anthony sensed fear in her voice. Fear of death—fear of never obtaining her inheritance! If she escaped the former—Jim would see to it that, unfortunately, the object of the latter fear was brought upon her. But she could kill him later. She would never give up in trying to do that as long as she stopped him from reaching that money.

For now, however, Jim and Tom were the ones who had to focus on escape!

Anne's terror made her desperate, and with the strength of ten she bolted for the elevator. This strength mostly went into shoving aside both Tom Gentry and Jim Anthony—a feat that almost none had accomplished. Only the circumstances put them off-balance enough. Before they knew it the elevator was ascending!

Behind them stood only the possibility of quick and complete destruction. But the elevator shaft yawned open ahead of them, and they had to *try*, if nothing else. Jim Anthony didn't give up easily, and he'd protect Tom Gentry with his last breath. "Run, Tom!" he yelled. There was no fear in his voice—only a determination to survive against all odds.

Tom had to trust Jim when they fell into the shaft. At once Jim's mighty arm sprung out and his strong hand seized the cable. The rough exterior sliced it open as he gripped it—he winced and grunted, but held on, knowing he'd rather hurt his hand than be hurt beyond repair. Tom was able to seize the detective's ankle, and great strength was required to hang onto the cable while also keeping the pilot from fallen to a gruesome end, splattered to sauce at the base of the shaft. "I'm going to grab the cable, let's climb up!" Tom yelled.

"No, we have to wait!"

Tom didn't get a chance to tell "Wait for what?!" Heat had accumulated in the storage room, and with a pulse of flame that was the envy of any volcano, a sight that only Dante could describe—the Greek fire, and its maker, Alexander Kallinikos, the Flame Wizard, were no more.

Jim's ears were ringing, but Tom, being further below, was shielded for the most part from the deafening bang of the explosion. "*Holy God!*"

Tom rarely said such a thing, and indeed Jim Anthony couldn't remember if he had ever said it before. But this was an exciting life for a pilot, and always elicited any number of bombastic words! It was good for a thrill-seeking man such as Tom Gentry to live a life at the side of Jim Anthony.

"Now we climb," Jim said. Slowly, cautiously, the two men scaled the coarse wire of the elevator. The pulse of flame had been brief, however strong it may have been, and therefore the cables were hot but thankfully not melted. Still, neither of them wanted to stay here for very long—the explosion had likely destabilized most of the building, and the upper parts were far older than these lower levels. It could all fall in at any time that was to say, so time was of the essence! After all, there was the additional fact that Anne Somerset was escaping. Jim didn't doubt that she had pinched some of the Greek fire. She could use it again in her scheme to wipe out the rest of Sherman Financial! But the climb back up was very long, and since they had to go slow, even powerful men like themselves were exhausted.

Still, Jim's stamina recovered quickly. "Go on without me, Jim!" Tom had urged. And Jim had said nothing in reply. Tom Gentry then wandered out in the streets of Heraklion, and, after sighing heavily, wondered if there was a place where his money was good enough to buy a drink.

Jim had no time for such thoughts, were he ever prone to them. His mighty legs were pumping, to follow a sight which equally mighty eyes had spotted. Anne was escaping across a nearby field, but there was no way in Hell she was faster than him.

• • •

Heavy thumping footsteps hit the packed mud—soft from the Mediterranean fog that covered the island, but still stiff. Or perhaps Jim Anthony was running too fast for the mud to grip him. The heavy weight of his bones, his muscles, made Anne hear him coming from far behind. And over an open field like this, unless he tripped over a hidden rock, nothing could stop him from reaching her. And he certainly wasn't going to trip over any rocks.

She got ready to fight. It wasn't her first fight, and she'd proven to herself time and time again—challenging men who crept out of bars, or who were drunk in alleyways—that she could handle anyone. Perhaps the legendary Jim Anthony would be the heated contest she wanted!

But despite what she'd seen of him, and despite his great record, she wondered if there was anything to him against a *real* opponent. Maybe he, like so many of her unwitting sparring partners, was afraid to hit a lady. She could definitely use that against him. It was a terrific advantage in so many situations. But above all else, he was rich, like those she hated—and that made him soft in her eyes.

Of course, maybe there didn't need to be a brawl in the first place. Maybe she could just shoot him!

She pulled a six-barreled magnum out of her pants pocket, and aimed it squarely at the fast approaching Jim Anthony. She fired, taking time to be accurate between shots—she anticipated each dodge and weave he made to escape the bullets. He'd evaded the sniper in headquarters, after all, so there was only a small chance she'd hit him...and a smaller one that the shot would kill him.

Six bullets weren't enough. But again, she'd be ready. She was *always* ready! She'd been prepared for Jim Anthony leading an assault on the Flame Wizard before the Flame Wizard himself even got his start. He would have been *easily* wiped out if she hadn't been there, and he'd still been foolish to the bitter end. Now Jim Anthony was almost upon her. She pulled out a knife from her belt, and slung it at him once he was close enough. Again, like the hammer coming down on her pistol, he snapped out of the way before the weapon stood a chance of interrupting his path. He was close—close enough to jump! He lunged at her, and they began to grapple—!

At first, she nearly got him with the dagger, which whipped through the air with a sharp *zip*. He sidestepped and aimed a bone-crushing blow at her torso...only to see her own arm, her free one, snap up to deflect. Another attempt to stab—this time she seized his wrists, yanking one of his arms away while he seized her wrist. Without a rush of strength the fatal jab would pierce his heart!

He raised a leg to kick her, but in surprise found that she kept her balance while also kicking away his own leg. The sheer ability she displayed caused his other leg to buckle, and he collapsed. In doing so, though, he slung her over him, and tossed her into a crumpled pile!

The knife was far away from them, and she tried to go for it. Jim Anthony's foot struck out again, so much like a desert snake. He caught the photographer's ankle and pulled her down. But she rolled even as he stood up, and she tried to tackle him down again. When this failed there was an attempt on both ends to flatten each other with haymakers. Jim Anthony *didn't* hold back against women if he had to! And she could take all of it. Her eyes never lost that blazing hatred, that impetus to kill.

In fact, a blow to the gut crumpled up even the powerful Irish-Indian. With him thus paralyzed, she was free to go back to get the knife, almost dancing as she did so. She laughed as she picked it off the ground, and reached once more into her pocket, her laughter echoing across the plains. She removed a thick glass vial containing the trademark grey pellets of the Flame Wizard. "I can find another chemist to recreate this formula," she cackled. "Maybe I don't need to stop at killing the board members—maybe I can worm my way into some *real* power. Now I won't be stuck taking peanuts for photos of dead bodies! And my poor mother, she'll finally achieve the pretty things that her brother should have given her!"

"Anne, I keep telling you, none of this will work!" Jim yelled. "Kallinikos used the *Rosa fragor* to create the Greek fire—that species is officially extinct! If the last specimens of it weren't blown up with the rest of that floor, the secret of their location was lost with him!" He didn't even need to say that outside of the mystique of it all, the Greek fire was little more than a miniaturized explosive—there were other weapons stronger than it—and there would be even more terrible ones soon enough.

But then he noticed another detail—his eyes widened with horror. "Look out, Anne!" he yelled. The afternoon sun was glimmering on the dagger. The reflection shined bright through the glass of the Greek fire vial. Like frying ants with a magnifying glass...heat would be focused on the chemical pellets!

Already the grey was yielding to yellow-hot. Anne Somerset's eyes locked on the vial. Her painted lips began to move to voice some sort of cry when Greek fire burned for the last time.

Her death must have been instantaneous. The fire was so hot that even her bones burnt to nothing but ashes.

Jim Anthony watched in horror—it had all happened so fast. "Ashes to ashes, and dust to dust, Anne," he said. He spoke the words without a trace of mockery or irony.

But at last it was all over. The murderers had seen justice. And Jim Anthony was, as the antique seller Isabella had said, a man of great heart. He pitied Alexander Kallinikos, even if he had caused his own woes, and he saw a great deal of potential in Anne Somerset—if only they had not been consumed by their own obsessions, they may given something truly wonderful to the world.

Wearily, he walked to the edge of the plains, and sat cross-legged on the shores of the bobbing Cretan sea.

End of Part One

MURDER HAS
BLUE SCALES

It was one of those low Arizona sunsets that any artist would dream of seeing. The orange, time-scarred stones of the desert were beginning to cast low shadows, making every crack in the rocks, on the chapped sandy floor, an eerie jack-o-lantern spectacle. Lizards scampered across the dry ground and sometimes if one wasn't paying attention, these tiny scratches would sound like the footsteps of someone sneaking up on them.

On a night like this, the cool October of 1937, it was best to stay indoors—say, at something like a Halloween party. That was exactly what was happening inside the looming palace of Baron Berger Sturm, late of Bavaria. He'd had it specially built here in the Mojave, in imitation of the famous detective he'd heard of, even in his native land: Jim Anthony. Indeed, Jim Anthony's famous Pueblo was said to be in the Mojave, not far at all from the high superstructure of Castle Sturm.

Many of the guests of the Castle were not personal friends of the Baron. The Baron's friends came and went, and so his functions were always to encourage the creation of a new (fragile) social circle. Thus they were open to the public, and many people from Arizona, Nevada, and even California came, just to see a real castle, and a real European aristocrat. This time around the Baron was offering a special treat for anyone who attended this particular get-together—he had just made the discovery of an underground lake below the foundation of Castle Sturm! He had hired a team of miners to dig out what was to be a new wing in the sub-basement when suddenly they came across the great cavern that contained what the Baron called in his own words...

"...the purest crystal-clear lake in all the world." Below a well-formed mustache, he smiled broadly as his guests, all clad in a variety of costumes representing creatures of the night, released a collective gasp. The cave chamber was dank and poorly lit, but the glowing blue waters of the massive lake would have astonished even visitors to the Pueblo of Jim Anthony. The Baron himself was dressed as a vampire, wearing a bat-winged mask to cast a shadow over his odd yellow eyes—which did not appear to be the product of colored contacts.

It was not as if the guests of Baron Sturm had not already seen dazzling sights upon receiving a tour of the Castle. The entrance, and all the rooms set to receive guests, were full of extraordinarily rare pieces by artists of any and every century of human history. There were some of the Baron's own creations there as well—giant, clumsy, experimental things. The word "giant," of all the descriptors given to these pieces, was the most relevant. The lengths the Baron went to in making his creations larger than life were second to none. This included the theatrical personality with which he shocked the senses of his newfound friends.

The party attendees had not noticed the large steel fire-door that had been installed in the entrance to the cavern of the lake. In the entryway was a switch which could seal this door in an instant. It could resist even the highest caliber of bullets—whenever this door was dropped; there was nothing that could be done from the end without a set of controls. As Baron Sturm considered this fact, he hoped it would not come down to using this door.

The guests crowded close to the lake, and the Baron was able to count them for the first time. They numbered around forty. It was a good crowd.

One of the men was the first to cry out. "Look!" he said, pointing. "There's—there's something bubbling in the lake!"

"Dear friends," the Baron said, his Bavarian accent still prominent even after all the years of living in the States. "There are fish in the lake—after all; it is linked by a subterranean passage to the Pacific Ocean! Do not be surprised!"

But the bubbles were massive, and soon all the guests were fixated on them, talking amongst themselves, speculating on where they were coming from. Some were already backing away, closer to the Baron, who stood near to the exit.

The bubbles then were replaced with a rush of displaced water—it was like a geyser, and for a second the guests were struck with the horrific notion that there was some sort of volcanic activity underwater. But the truth was far worse. Once the water cleared it was obvious that there was a figure swimming towards the party—it was a humanoid, but not *human*. Indeed, it seemed to be *blue*—a darker blue than the waters it swam in, to be sure. The blue was the colors of the scales that covered it. It was a humanoid *fish*, evidenced by the heaving gills on its neck, which sat below a head hideous beyond reckoning—the glassy nebulous eyes reflected a terrible inhumanity. Worst of all, however, were the long fingers, which terminated with long, savage claws!

The response in the crowd was visceral—ancestral. The bestial impulse and ability to recognize predators awoke in all of them, and like a flock of startled cattle they stampeded to escape back into the basement—to evade this horrible, wretched creature!

The blue-scaled horror was out of the water when Baron Berger Strum expressed his fear of the creature for the first time. As he dove through the exit door, screaming, he seized the door controls and slammed the fire-door shut. "Baron! Baron!" many of the guests screamed. "There are still people out there!"

Siblings, spouses, parents and children—half the entire party was trapped with that thing! Twenty souls, lost to the claws of that barbarian creature!

Though the thickness of the door may have been impossible to breach, some sound still came through it. However, these sounds were little more than the tortured screams of the damned people imprisoned with the monster! People pounded on the door, and on the Baron, to make him open the door, damn their own lives—they'd face the monster rather than lose the others. But the Baron screamed out, "The lever is *broken*! I cannot open it!"

And most of the crowd bolted upstairs, to escape the dying shrieks that still echoed through the door. One man announced he was going to call the police, but he was later found dead—apparently having thrown himself down a flight of stairs in grief.

The Baron was the one who contacted the police. When they finally drove out through the desert, they had a technician with them to get the fire-door open. The officers that found what awaited within were sent, with the remaining party guests, to a Nevadan mental hospital for a prolonged stay. The breakdowns of their sanity were absolute and total.

Baron Strum was allowed to stay in his castle, but under house arrest. His house was cleaned up once the crime scene was processed, but no one on the police force was willing to check into the mysterious lake that was the home of the azure-fleshed monster.

Of course, it was decided after a short discussion to go through a little-used page of their phone-book. The call went out to a private line—in the Pueblo, stronghold of Jim Anthony!

• • •

Jim Anthony was not in the Pueblo, however—he was in the Teepee. Cross-legged, bare-footed, he was deep in meditation. He was recovering from his wounds from his last case, where he went up against the sinister Flame Wizard, the master of Greek fire. Bodily, he was fine—merely a little exhausted. Yet the case had left a psychological strain. Despite his descent from the proud and determined Comanche Fawn Johntom and her husband, brave, devil-may-care Irish explorer Shean Boru Anthony, he was still mortal, and subject to stress. But with his sharp mind and the power of meditation, he would soon be his old self again. Which was a good thing, to be sure! His sixth sense, which foretold danger, was burning deep in his skull, and therefore even without knowledge of the fine details, he was sensing the faraway murders in the mysterious Castle Sturm.

As he stood, he began to leave his private quarters, hearing the radio go off in the other room. "Calling Jim Anthony! Calling Jim Anthony!" Anthony grinned as he heard the voice of his aged grandfather, Mephito. He and some of the employees at the Pueblo were trying to relay the message of the police.

"What's going on, Grandfather? Over," Jim Anthony.

"There is great trouble coming, my son. One of our number here says that you are required in this land."

"In Arizona? I understand. I'll take a plane at once. Over."

"It sounds urgent, my son! Please hurry."

"I will. Over and out."

Jim Anthony did hesitate for a moment, deliberately being slow in setting down the microphone, but again, he was mortal. His body was tensing up, in an attempt to *squeeze* out the pain and tension. It was working—the call to action was fuel to him; it was balm. Adventure could regenerate parts of him that were broken. And so the trauma of his previous case melted away. Again, he was needed. And so he would sally forth again, like an ancient knight!

Soon, the *Thunderbird* was flying free from the Teepee, brought there in the first place by its pilot, the tough Irishman called Tom Gentry. He, too, was exhausted from the fight against the Flame Wizard—he had been there, fighting alongside the detective in thick and thin. But still, he had a great loyalty to Jim Anthony, and therefore could ignore the handicaps adventuring inflicted. They would fade in time, naturally.

The flight was silent. The last time they'd flown together they'd been talkative, but that seemed a distant memory now. They both wanted to reach Arizona quickly. In the meantime, Jim opened radio communications with the Kingman Police.

"Jim Anthony, thank you for coming," an officer was saying. "We'll have a car ready at the airport to take you to Castle Sturm, plus a warrant for you to search the premises. We've placed Baron Sturm in custody."

"That sounds good, sir," Anthony replied. "We'll find out what this... fish-monster is. We have to initially assume it's just a clever crook, rather than some sort of supernatural beast."

"I hope you're right, Anthony. I hope you're right..."

Jim did nothing to betray his own feelings on the matter. He wanted to leave his deductions to his in-person senses, rather than his imagination— for indeed, a strong imagination was a powerful tool of a good detective, but also a great enemy at times.

The *Thunderbird* was one of the fastest things in the sky and so it was a quick flight from the Catskills to the Mojave. The scarlet sands were always so alluring to Jim, even though he came here often to stop over at the Pueblo. He liked, when he had time to do so, to walk into the desert and observe the depth of nature. Even in what seemed to be just a barren wasteland, there was life—the small green plants, and the small green lizards. The insects and arachnids. Jim's people from his Native American side, the Comanche, had lived in New Mexico. Though Arizona was largely Navajo territory, the American desert in general had sentimental value to him through the sense of belonging it gave him with his Comanche kin.

When the plane touched down, Jim went to the cabin to check on Tom. The sturdy pilot was leaning heavily on the controls, and was breathing heavily—but in a tranquil manner. It was the breathing of someone right on the edge of sleep. He smiled warmly. "Rest up, Tom. I'll take it from here."

"Jim, no, that—that won't be..." But he never finished that sentence. Jim's smile only widened.

After checking to make sure the plane was properly locked down, the detective descended the exit ramp where already the comforting sight of a police car could be seen. Several of the Kingman officers were approaching the plane.

"Thanks again, Jim Anthony," a familiar voice said. "I'm Officer Arn Benjamin. I'm in charge of the Castle Sturm case. You see, we, uh, don't really have people besides officers and the chief. And the chief has other business to attend to. Something about people vanishing in the South Pacific..."

Jim realized how dour his face was, and he cracked a smile. "I understand, Officer Benjamin. Let's get over to Castle Sturm right away."

Once he got in the police car, Benjamin's partner, who only identified as "Louis," offered him some coffee. It was much appreciated on Anthony's behalf, even if it was cheap and weak.

The drive to Castle Sturm from Kingman wasn't a long one, but nonetheless, even from the airport, the silhouette of their destination against the desert sky could be seen. Jim Anthony had seen castles before, but it was still a sublime and unique sight to see the spires of Castle Sturm rise out of the flats of the Mojave. It had an artificial plateau built under it, so that it could even have an authentic moat. Stocked with crocodiles, no less! But the beasts had been tamed, and obviously, no one was meant to be thrown in. It was all part of Baron Sturm's performative nature. Something about their absent host rubbed Anthony the wrong way, though. He couldn't put his finger on it. As he debated it with himself, however, he realized he had started talking under his breath—a shocking loss of his usual self-control.

"What's that about the Germans, Anthony?" Officer Benjamin asked.

"Oh. Yes. I was contemplating an old question."

"And which old question would that be?"

Jim chuckled lightly. "'Where was he during the War?'"

"A good thing to ask. But Baron Sturm moved to the United States twenty-five years ago, before the War started—or so he says."

Jim went silent. There were several branching possibilities in the words of the policeman.

The car crossed the drawbridge after climbing the ramp onto the artificial plateau. This drawbridge was kept lowered while the investigation was ongoing. Inside the massive castle there was a parking lot—if such a thing could be believed!—where already several squad cars were stationed.

Even Jim Anthony had to admit to his senses being stunned by the hugeness of the place. It was almost a fairy-tale world, something that one could only dream about. Baron Sturm wasn't just rich; he was *fabulously* wealthy. But to Jim's mind, it meant an increased chance of one probability...

A man with this much wealth would have an equivalent amount of power. Power to do whatever he wanted!

Jim exited the car and turned to Officer Benjamin, with efficiency and speed on his mind. "I want to be taken to the chamber where it happened. If I can't find anything there, I'll know how hard to search the rest of the castle."

Benjamin was able to move at a pace swift enough to accommodate Jim's normal walking pace. Jim was naturally very tall and much of his height came from his long legs—and in any case his sense of priority kept him moving. It was awkward and even somewhat painful to walk at the pace that most people took, and so he was glad that Benjamin had both his stamina and his values.

Again, he was caught off-guard by the splendor of the sight that greeted him, once they descended into the Castle's inner recesses by means of a large stone-cut Grand Staircase: the cave was almost absurdly massive, and the lake was indeed of some of the most beautiful water anyone had ever seen. The space was artificially carved, of course. It was easy to recognize via the geometric cuts along each of the walls. That was a point against the Baron, who claimed the cave existed naturally and that he had discovered it. It was manufactured, alright—but he couldn't imagine that there was any sort of underwater passage. Building such a thing—a full-on connection to the Pacific Ocean—would be ludicrously expensive. The "fish-monster" probably just hid in an underwater chamber, or deep enough in the water so that he could not be seen—and Anthony used the word "he" because, as he had said, it was likely just an ordinary person in a suit, armed with breathing equipment.

He was carrying a suitcase containing the appropriate gadgets. There was one he had in mind that was specially tailored to a situation like this— a motor-powered sonar device that could operate by remote control. A special radio band that Jim had discovered could control it at an almost unlimited range. It was still something of a prototype, and Jim didn't know if he'd have a chance to use it again after this. The devices of Jim's arsenal were virtually limitless in number and specificity, as the detective predicted every eventuality with a borderline paranoia—and yet all the same, some of them turned out to be wastes of time. But for now he was going to use it to explore the dimensions of this lake.

He barely noticed that both Arn Benjamin and Louis had exited the chamber almost immediately after showing him to the room. He hadn't had the energy to exposit his plan to them—not today, at least—so it was nice that they stayed out of his hair. He lowered the probe into the water, and took out the remote control panel. Water could ordinarily block radio waves, but the frequency he used was capable of overcoming that. Already he could see, through a small screen on the controller, that the lake was not incredibly deep. There was a small chamber, which Jim believed—or wanted to believe—was just a small alcove. But as he sent the probe into this space, it did seem to go back quite a-ways. He tensed as the probe began to confirm what he believed to be impossible—there *was* a passage

"I want to be taken to the chamber..."

that had been dug out! How far could it possibly go?

Anthony set the drone to continue moving forward at a uniform speed. And it moved unimpeded, for miles and miles. The detectives felt sweat break out on his brow. It was scarcely believable—could this passage really lead into a larger body of water, where perhaps a *colony* of unknown humanoid creatures was waiting...?

No. That was too fantastic. For now.

But he did remember a handful of accounts he looked over when he had a chance to examine some rare manuscripts at some of the many great universities he had attended. Oftentimes "supernatural" was a word people inserted to make up for a lack of vocabulary for the indescribable—culture and cultural images couldn't keep up with these encounters with the unknown. Jim Anthony thus did believe that science had its limits, even if he hoped someday there would be *almost* no unknowns. And so among the tales of the unknowns he had studied, there had been one of monsters such as these. Piscean humanoids could be found in the stories of mermaids—they were far from new.

It would be easy to write this off as nothing but old wives' tales, urban folklore. But Jim wasn't swayed. All the same, his probe was still moving. Soon it would be out of the limits of Arizona. It was traveling through Nevada en route to California—and then, maybe to the Pacific Ocean, as the Baron had said!

Jim wanted to wait a few hours before takeoff, so that Tom could sleep, but he still intended to return to the plane in the meantime. That way he could work in a familiar space as he checked to make sure if there were any significant places the tunnel passed under.

His memory failed to remind him that his police escorts had wandered off. He returned to the parking garage before realizing that he would need one of them to drive him back to the *Thunderbird*. He was about to turn back (as he had stepped onto the drawbridge) when something caught the edge of his eye.

It was only after a drowsy second had passed that he realized the thing in his peripheral vision—descending the wall of the castle, like some sort of scuttling vermin—was blue. Like the scales of the monster he'd been warned of!

Jim Anthony turned, and his eyes widened. There, with claws sunk deep into the hard stone of the wall, was the fish-man!

● ● ●

His primeval face was split with what looked like the grin of a monstrous clown, with the skinny spines of teeth jutting out from the pale blue gums. A barbed tongue thrashed inside the monster's mouth, and its dead-looking eyes flashed with a sadistic intelligence. For a second its stare seemed to mock Anthony. Then, with what Anthony could only call grace, it dived deep into the moat!

Anthony knew he had to pursue the creature into the water. Benjamin had told him that Sturm had "tamed" the crocodiles, but Anthony knew he had to be prepared for them to nonetheless attack an intruder. All the same, he seemed to remember going up against some of these reptilian beasts in the past. He just had to remember to stay calm—and bury his fear of them. He didn't fear them, because he had faith in his abilities.

And those abilities had carried him far—now they took him far below the surface of the moat. His eyes adjusted fast into the darkness of the water, as he had trained them to do so no matter what the nature of the darkness was. But at once, he realized he couldn't see his quarry—even if something was disturbing the silt at the moat's bottom. Through the clouds of mud they kicked up, he could see them. They were the crocodiles, and they didn't look tame at all—rather, they looked as if they'd been deprived of food. Anthony felt pity for the animals, but sensed that he had been tricked somehow, in regards to making this dive. Now he had to make his escape!

He made a powerful stroke upward through the water, which was so unlike the crystal-clear stuff that his probe was still swimming through. A shudder passed through him, however, as he felt coarse scales brush against his exposed calf. He tried to swim slowly, but the ravenousness of the beasts meant his calm pace accounted for nothing. One of them was coming towards him now—its jaws wide open, revealing the endless rows of demonic fangs!

Like hooks they sank deep into Jim Anthony's calf. He cried out and lost some of his precious air. For many men, this would be the end—that solitary moment where they were lost forever. Blood was filling the water. There was so much that it drifted upward past Anthony's bleary eyes. But the sight of blood was enough to once again reinvigorate the detective. He had been careless in jumping down here—his exhaustion had caught up to him much more than he'd ever wanted to admit. Still, he had enough energy to realize there was a reason for that. If he survived the lizards, he'd have time to contemplate it further.

In a flash he snapped down to pull the reptile's teeth out of his leg, by seizing the creature's snout and jaw, and pulling. No less than five others were joining their brother from the darkness. As his lungs burned, the mighty muscles that flexed in those tights arms did not weaken. He was free in moments, and made another desperate lunge for the surface. He was almost there when another of the beasts was about to outflank him. They weren't dumb brutes: they knew he would need air, just as they did. They were accustomed to this water—nature had bred them to hold their breaths far longer than humans. But Jim Anthony had done something similar. Another thrust and fresh air was in his mouth! His vision was clearing now, and he wanted to reach the castle wall so he could scale it and get back on track. There was a thrust below the water ahead of him, through, and two of the crocs were upon him!

Even though the air was sweeter than ambrosia on Olympus, Jim Anthony dove again, this time to sneak below the close-treading animals. They were fast for their size, but again—so was he. His hair, drifting in the water, tickled the bellies of the lizards. He needed to still be relatively close to the surface, so he could rise quickly. In fact he thrust himself into the air not unlike a dolphin. No one was there to witness it but the crocodiles. His muscles were entirely conditioned to his will—he could surpass any limit with their strength, and that final jolt from the croc's bite had empowered him with all the excellence he'd need to face down the mysterious blue-scaled monster.

His fingertips clung to the rocky surface of the side of the magnificent structure. Unlike the fish-man, he had no claws with which to secure his grip, but if he fell again he would never get out. Or so he told himself. The threat of death—without the *fear* of death—was a strong motivator. Jim Anthony laughed in the face of death, or at least snickered when it wasn't paying attention. And he loved life, as a natural part of himself. He would not let it go—not while he still had a fight left in him.

Soon he was on the drawbridge once more, the dark wood becoming stained with his oozing blood. The various vaccines and medications he had taken ensured that the wound wouldn't become infected, so it was really a minor annoyance—it would become even less of one once he got bandages and maybe a brace on the leg. (He probably really wouldn't need a brace. Jim Anthony could still go for a light jog even if one of his legs was fractured.) He was thinking of his tiredness, which had crept in the background and caused him to hallucinate the monster. It must have been the coffee! It had been intended to invigorate him, but instead it only made him more careless. It may have induced hallucinations, because clearly the fish-person was never in the water! It couldn't have swum fast enough to get away from Anthony in the time it took for him to join it.

His thought shifted to the officer he had met with: Officer Arn Benjamin. Benjamin, Arn...a pun took shape in Jim Anthony's mind, involving an infamous figure from the dawn of United States history—whose name had become a common title for betrayers. "Good Lord," he said aloud then. "What a coincidence!" He'd noticed the cosmic joke of the name before and had been privately amused by it, but now it seemed Benjamin was out to earn his name as a genuine Ben Arnold.

So there was a mole in the Police Department assigned to this case. Anthony's mind carried little doubt that this was due to the great wealth of Baron Sturm. Sturm was indeed a deadly foe. He knew that the answers would lie wherever the probe ended up. Back to the *Thunderbird* it was, then, to continue to keep an eye on the probe's location. Tom Gentry was still sleeping but Anthony knew he would awaken soon. With his own energy back he was able to lock his eyes on the scanner.

After a few hours, the probe stopped moving. It was in San Francisco. That was where Sturm's impossible tunnel led!

• • •

When Tom Gentry awoke, Jim explained the entire situation to him.

"Holy Gee-man-ee!" he cried. "A traitorous policeman—what a terrible shame. That bad money of Baron Sturm's is heavy stuff."

"Agreed, Tom," Jim Anthony said. "So we need to head to San Francisco at once."

"Jet lag, my friend—beware it!" But Jim only grinned in response. Tom grinned with him. "I'm just glad that there's an official airport in 'Frisco. Been awhile since we've been to one of those, it seems. I hope your drone shows the right place, Jim!"

Jim took one of his now-familiar silences. They took off in a hurry, and when they were in the sky, Jim felt more at ease. They were on their way to busting this nonsense—even if it wasn't nonsense at all. Murder was nonsensical, it was true, but unlike most nonsense, there was a deadly lack of humor in the whole thing. And Jim's mind was still in conflict over the true nature of the weird creature he had seen—and that the relatives of that terrible wave of victims had seen. Hallucinations caused by drugs could not kill unless they caused the person, in their desire to flee, to kill themselves by accident. But they could enhance the appearance of a man in a suit. Even a fake-looking costume would become shocking and terrible in the eyes of somehow who was unaware they were given such a dreadful narcotic!

Once again the *Thunderbird* provided itself to be a king of speed, and soon enough the flight to 'Frisco was over. Using a function on the scanner, Jim was able to pinpoint the map coordinates of the probe's location. Members of the various organizations he led had secured a rental car for him in the airport's parking lot, and once Tom picked up the keys they climbed in. Looking over a local map he'd gotten at the airport, Jim said: "It looks like we're heading towards a warehouse!"

"I don't think these fishy beasts would use a warehouse as their secret base," Tom admitted.

Once again Jim Anthony was silent. This time, however, he was lost in neutral thoughts, rather than negative ones.

They closed in on the warehouse, and Tom parked the car as inconspicuously as possible. There was a chance the place was guarded. Jim gestured for Tom to come with him, which he was very eager to do—"Still kicking myself for napping on the job!" he said. He'd get to sate his lust for action soon enough!

Slowly, they crept up on what appeared to be a backdoor for the employees. Jim Anthony took a skeleton key from his pocket, and swiftly unlocked the door. Holding back all noise, they got inside.

The warehouse was full of shelves that were stacked high with wooden crates. There wasn't a lot of free space in here, and Jim knew at once that there were many places for enemies to hide—his sixth sense was a strong pointer towards confirmation of that suspicion. And indeed, once both men were well within the premises...

SLAM. Their entrance was sealed, from a man who was hiding behind the door. A man with a gun at the ready!

In truth there were several such men, all stepping from behind one thing or another. Soon Tom and Jim were completely surrounded by this group of serious-looking hoodlums clad in fine pinstripe suits. One of them was carrying a shotgun, and as Jim Anthony raised his hands he looked the detective dead in the eye.

"So dis is the great Jim Anthony, huh?" he asked. "Don't look so big to me, fella. And yer about to get a heckuva lot smaller..."

"After you blow me to chunks, I presume?" Anthony replied, his face as stoic as ever.

"Dat's the idea, yeah."

"And I don't suppose you can bother to tell me who you're working for?"

"Nuh-uh, Anthony. I'm not one of the big smart dudes you run up against, who talks his head off 'bout what he's up to. I'm just a hard working man who got into this biz to keep up with some regular exercise. Just listening to my doctor, you know?"

Jim Anthony didn't have any wise words about doctors, but he could introduce this crook to a maxim of Archimedes: with a lever, one can move the world. And the barrel of the shotgun was basically just a big lever. Jim seized the barrel and pulled down hard, counting on the man's grip to tighten from surprise. As usual his prediction came true, and thus Jim was able to flip the man head over heels, which planted him sprawled on the ground—unconscious.

"Ho-lee...!" came a cry. The speaker of this was soon out too, in less than a second. In that hanging moment there had been two cannon bursts as the mighty muscles of Jim Anthony pumped out two swings, a right and a left. Suddenly three of the men were on the ground.

Tom Gentry was inspired. "Way to go, Jim!" he cried out, before he whirled to deck the man on his left. It was a mighty blow, but he didn't have Jim's reflexes, and so was in grave danger.

"Look out, Tom!" Jim started to cry, as the guns blazed. He was about to grapple with another of the men, but if he didn't move, Tom was a dead man. He knocked the chauffeur to the ground just as the shots rang out. His speed evaded the bullets and with a spinning kick, three more men were on the ground.

There were two others still standing and Jim realized he'd left his back open to them. He could get *one*, but not both...

But suddenly he heard one of the survivors slip and collapse with a cry. When he turned to face the source of this sound—and his remaining target—he saw that Tom, even while prone, had carried on the fight by jerking out the man's ankle from under him. The last standing foe, seeing the resourcefulness of the champions of justice, had sweat trickling down his forehead, and soon that forehead was creased from a final punch.

Tom staggered to his feet.

"There really isn't anything that can stop you, is there, Jim?" the chauffeur said, slapping his friend on the back.

"Maybe, but I don't have a lead now," Jim replied bitterly. "This was just another trap by whoever's behind this."

"Let's search a little bit. Maybe—" Tom never got to finish his sentence. He was interrupted by the unmistakable sound of an ear-splitting shriek!

The sound could be heard in the direction of the far end of the warehouse. There was a window there, and when Tom saw the window he knew what Jim Anthony was about to do. There was no stopping the man when anyone was in danger. Of course, it may have helped that the voice was clearly female.

Tearing off his shirt to wrap around his arm, Jim's running pace didn't decrease at all. And he regained his velocity instantly even after he dove through the window—shielding himself with his wrapped arm as the glinting blades of glass danced in the air around him.

He noticed at once that he had landed on the beachfront. A storm was rising, and so the California beaches were uncommonly deserted—but the sign of trouble was clear ahead. A blonde woman, clearly unaware or uncaring of the coming weather, was collapsed on the sand. One arm was futilely raised as if an attempt to stop something dreadful from happening. Jim was able to see that she was very lovely—and though fear blazed in her eyes now, she had a face of courage. She was startled when Jim landed on the sands beside her. He helped her to her feet, and she clung to his arm like her life depended on it. So much so that her nails bit into his skin.

"What's the matter?" he asked hurriedly.

"My friend and I were out swimming, when this...monster came up to us!" she cried. And she turned to point along the length of the beach. "You can still see it!"

Indeed, there it was in the distance—the familiar cerulean scales of the fish-monster! Relatively unimpeded, it was running down the beach, though it was too far for even the well-honed eyes of Jim Anthony to see who exactly the beast was carrying. He remembered the butchery in the cave and knew that another innocent life was at stake—he was to be the only barrier between the unfortunate kidnapee and a bloody, agonizing death!

When adrenaline hit Jim Anthony it had an even stronger effect than it did on normal men. Indeed, even a seasoned biker would be challenged to keep up with the crime-fighter's sprint. But as he neared the creature, it glanced over its shoulder and began to run faster. It was running out of beach, however, but it scrambled up onto a nearby boardwalk and continued from there. Jim wouldn't need to waste time *climbing* the boardwalk—just a sturdy *leap* and...

And the creature was gone.

Jim stopped in his tracks. He would have rubbed his eyes if he thought it would have done any good at all. But indeed, after a few seconds of staring, he confirmed that the thing that had climbed the boardwalk had entirely disappeared.

• • •

When Jim walked back, Tom was talking to the girl in a raised voice while gesturing wildly. Upon seeing Jim approach he breathed a sigh of relief. "I was wondering where you'd got to, Jim," he said. "And she's too hysterical to—"

"Tom, that's a terrible thing to say. This young woman's friend was just kidnapped by our prey."

"...which I was *attempting* to explain to him!" the lady cried. "But say—your name is Jim? You wouldn't happen to be that 'super-detective' that I've heard of, Jim Anthony?"

"I'm Jim Anthony, yes. Can I ask your name, miss?"

"I'm Linda Carlyle. I was practicing my swimming for the 1940 Olympics."

"That's a noble goal!" Jim said. "But I'm sorry that I—couldn't save your friend."

"What even happened out there?" she asked. Her voice was suddenly full of a deep concern. "I couldn't see far enough to tell."

"Well, Miss Carlyle, they—vanished."

"Vanished?" Linda and Tom exclaimed this simultaneously.

"Yes. This isn't the first time the creature's gotten away from me, Ms. Carlyle. Perhaps it can turn invisible. I cannot afford to rule out any possibilities."

"Wait! You've *met* this creature before?!"

Jim took some time to explain the situation. "And I believe this entity has its home in this area. And there may be others," he said when he was done.

Linda didn't seem too pleased with that prospect. "Well, my friend is still out there somewhere!" she said. "Invisibility or not, and plural creatures or not, I want to go find her!"

Jim grinned. Her tenacity was admirable. "Would you at least accept the help of Tom and I?" he said.

"I've heard good things about you, Mr. Anthony," Linda replied. "I'd find it a personal pleasure."

Pleasure was a curious word for her to use—for once again, Jim Anthony was finding himself getting carried away with certain thoughts and fancies. Even in her disheveled state, Linda Carlyle had a very obvious natural beauty. Her swimming practices had left a heavy tan on her skin, which largely shrouded packs of barely visible freckles on her neck and shoulders. Her blonde hair stretched down a great length of her long back, and her almost-too-small swimsuit was of the same shimmering blue as her eyes. The sheer amount of skin she was showing was a matter of obvious temptation to Anthony. He found the normal "strategy centers" of his brain becoming as liquid as the water they stood beside, and his vision blurred like ocean fog.

"Let's get going, then!" he said, trying to stop himself from stuttering. "We can use the rented car. There's no time to lose!"

And so the trio, led by Jim Anthony, began the dash back to the car. Tom hopped in the driver's seat while Jim took the back. But to his surprise, Linda sidled up along beside him. "Ms. Carlyle, you can take the front..." Jim suggested helpfully.

"That won't be necessary," she said. "I can see what's ahead just fine from back here." The detective at once sensed the double meaning of her words, by watching her eyes, as they traced up and down his body. He realized he was still shirtless, dressed only in his pants and leather Mexican sandals. Though humble, Jim Anthony had knowledge of the quality of his physique. All the same he hoped the droplets of sweat forming on him weren't visible.

The rented car barreled down the street parallel to the journey of the fish-monster, and as it did so, Linda's face immediately lit up. "Look, Jim!" she cried. "That—thing has some sort of slime coating! You can see its footsteps!"

The detective squinted out the window, and indeed, clearly defined on the road (from a point extending out from the boardwalk) he could see a thin green mucus forming the three-toed footprints of the monster. They were widely spaced, indicating its speed, but it wouldn't be able to outpace a car. Wordless, he leaned forward to keep track of where they were going. Even as he did, Linda yelled, "It looks like they turn off to the left!" They were coming up on an alley, and Jim's eyes confirmed what Linda's saw.

"Bank a left, Tom!" he said. "We may have it cornered—!"

"Careful, Jim," the driver returned. "It looks like a thin alleyway. There's a chance the car could get stuck..."

But he knew that Jim Anthony had a good handle on what he was doing. Even if the car *was* trapped, his instincts switched over to those of a wolf—every minute chance to survive could be capitalized in him.

And sure enough, by sheer velocity, the car forced its way between the two walls, yet stopped with a terrific jerk forward. "Tires are just spinning now!" Tom hollered. And with those words, Jim lunged for the roof of the car. In his hand was a knife of his own design, sharper than many available on the market. Even its edge wouldn't be able to cut a sizable enough hole in the roof of the vehicle in the time he needed, but he didn't require an entire hole. A flick of his wrists left a thick slash through the metal of the cabin. He made a sharp exhalation, and with his biceps tightening into footballs, he jammed his fingers into the incision. A quick yank down and he was free.

He knew the monster was out there even before he laid eyes on it. But even he felt a sense of nausea when he saw that Linda's friend wasn't with the beast—once again, he considered the plethora of terrible things it could have done to dispose of its victim. As it had before, it snarled at him, exposing those stalactites of evil teeth. Its muscles were nearly as tough-looking as his, and running down its belly was a lighter-colored strip of scales that seemed as hard as tank armor. It would be a brawl of the ages to take this thing down! Again, Jim Anthony flexed his muscles, and...

...and then a shot rang out!

Jim's reflexes saved him—by his thousands of hours of training he leaped, hoping sheer motion alone would save him from the bullet. But for the first time since his childhood, his ears had failed him, and even he hadn't had enough time to sense where the bullet was coming from. He let out a rare cry of agony as a chunk of meat was torn from his bulky calf.

He awkwardly slammed against the roof of the car and rolled down the windshield, towards the monster's waiting claws. As he did so, his vision covered in a faint redness from the pain, he heard another shot, and another cry, this time from a mouth besides his own. Tom Gentry had been shot!

Even as his powerful mind shunted away the torture creeping in his leg, Jim Anthony's vision remained clouded. Tom Gentry was his greatest companion—if he was ever forced, God forbid, to prize any of his associates above the others, it would be Tom. Even Gilgamesh and Enkidu couldn't hope to be as close as the two of them. If he was dead—a victim of the detective's eagerness—Jim would never forgive himself. He would be covered in a great shadow and his vengeance against evil would become even more terrible. It was this love that forced him to his feet, forced him to stand on an injury that few mortals could bear, and he peered into the cabin. Linda Carlyle was screaming, but her screams seemed distant to

Jim. He just wanted to see where Tom was hurt. At once, his dark eyes caught the sight of a small hole in his shoulder, from which blood was faintly leaking out. That there wasn't more blood meant the shooter had missed the brachial artery, which was a tremendous relief. The hulking Irish pilot was unconscious—but unconscious was better than dead.

Without considering what was behind him, Jim once again sank his fingers into the metal of the car, to begin shoving it out of the alley. The doors scraped loudly against the alley walls, and the sound rang in his ears even as his leg cried out for relief as he used it to push. But once it was out he delicately moved Tom over to the passenger seat and took the wheel himself. As he did so, he noticed the creature was gone. Perhaps the gunshots had frightened it off, and it escaped by climbing the wall as it had done at Castle Sturm. He didn't care for now—the creature had abandoned its kidnapping victim anyway, it seemed. He had quite forgotten about the kidnapping, not out of any insensitivity to the person involved, but out of his present all-eclipsing concern for Tom. Soon they were all back at the *Thunderbird*, and Jim spared no time in removing the bullet from the wound.

When he saw how shallow the wound was (comparatively), he breathed a sigh of relief—and remembered that Linda Carlyle was still with him. She seemed impressed by the interior of the *Thunderbird*—which was quite natural.

"He's going to be okay," Jim said at last. "No risk of infection, no significant blood loss. He just needs some rest."

"That's good," Linda murmured. She was still clearly shaken up from the gunshots, but so was Jim. He was slowly realizing he hadn't looked for the shooter, and he hadn't even examined the car to see where the shots had come from. It had been impulsive. He'd been losing focus all throughout the case, even as he'd dismissed the exhaustion from the previous one.

Only one way to rectify that. "I think we should head back out. Your friend isn't going to save...uh. Herself? Himself?"

"H-herself."

"Yes. I'm sorry, Linda, what's her name?"

She had been looking at the floor and glanced back up, and once again those eyes enchanted Jim Anthony. She glanced to the left, saying, "Peggy Travers." And her mouth dropped open somewhat then. "Jim, I...I know we haven't known each other very long...but..."

And suddenly, her arms were about his neck, and their lips met.

It seemed like awhile since a woman had kissed him—even if Anne, from his previous case, had taken the opportunity to make the move—and so he melted into the kiss's passion. Behind his closed eyes the world churned for him, and again he began to think fantastic thoughts about the future.

It wasn't easy for him to pull away from a kiss like that, but eventually he did, a faint smile visible on his mouth. Linda smiled back and his heart raced in his chest.

But then he tasted something on his lips. A chemical—certainly not the familiar faintness of lipstick. Linda took notice of his frown. "Is something wrong, Jim?" And her smile did not fade. Slowly, Jim began to realize it was a mocking smile. And with a mounting horror, he studied her fingernails and her lips. Both had an almost invisible sheen to them—indicating they'd been *coated* with something. Something that the kiss had entered into his system, and the scratches she given him when she clung to his arm on their first meeting. Anne Somerset had gotten him with poisoned nails too, but Linda was cleverer, or more vicious, adding the kiss into the mix.

The monster—at least in part—*was* the product of a hallucinogenic substance. The guests at Castle Sturm had been dosed with it—Officer Benjamin had likely given him some before he saw the creature on the side of the castle, and he was realizing that he only saw the monster when Linda had said something. Without her guiding presence, it had faded away just as it climbed the boardwalk. Tom hadn't seen the footprints because he was too busy driving the car—he'd listened to Jim when Linda had told him to see the footprints.

Linda noticed all of this going on in the detective's eyes, and her smile only widened. "Putting two and two together, I see, Mr. Super-Detective. It's a larger dose than usual, so you may be getting some additional side-effects."

Gradually, the light in the *Thunderbird* began to bend and twist curiously, though Jim tried to shove it from his eyes. Without meaning to, he held his hand up in front of his face, as if the hand, an avatar of his physical strength, could erase the infection. "You shot Tom," he accused.

"The gun is the only type of its kind—even you haven't dreamed of something so compact. I was able to conceal it in my bathing suit with ease and neither of you saw it coming! You didn't hear, because you weren't paying attention, but Tom was confused when you saw the creature and he didn't. He tried to stop me when I shot you, and I would've killed him, if I'd only been able to get in that second bullet!"

The detective's eyes were forced closed to a thin squint. "Who...are you?"

"I'm surprised that the great Jim Anthony didn't recognize the face of one of the deadliest mercenaries on the market," Linda hissed. Her head, it seemed to Jim, was weaving around like some sort of snake. "Ha! *I'm* Peggy Travers, you idiot. Margaret Travers, actually. There never was a friend kidnapped by the monster."

"Perhaps..." Jim began. His voice broke as everything in the room began to swirl and take on new fantastic colors. "Perhaps I haven't heard of you... because you have too high of regard for your own accomplishments."

The assassin smacked him across the face, though as his senses became flush with weird, overwhelming sensations, he barely felt it. "How *dare* you? Do you realize how hard it is to find work as a *female* mercenary in this backwards age? And one way or another, I *never* miss my target— never! Now you're completely within my power...helpless..." But an idea seemed to cross her mind. "But you're a handsome enough fellow. Maybe we can work out an agreement. The kiss *was* nice...and I'd enjoy taking you as my...paramour..."

The detective had to close his eyes at last to resist the churning hallucinations. But they persisted, even behind his eyelids. "I'd...never love... someone like you..."

But even as he said this, his eyes opened again, almost against his will. His thoughts and actions were no longer his own. And now, he was being assailed with a vision that threatened even his sanity—something beyond the horrible monsters of the mythologies of both his lineages. Linda—or Travers—had become like the cinematic vampire, or the Greek *lamia*, crossed with the Japanese *rokurokubi*. She had the slit-pupil eyes of a serpent, and the long, craning neck of that Japanese demon, covered in sickly-orange scales like an inverted version of the beast he sought. "You're— you're *not real!*" he cried. His voice shook somewhat but not from fear. "I-I know you're not. You told me you drugged me."

"But what if I *didn't?*" she shrieked. Her voice split the air like the banshees that prowled the homeland of Jim's father—proclaiming the legendary death-curse. He squeezed his hands tight against his ears to steel against the scream, but it was no use. The drug was too strong—! His body was crumpling from nausea, and he considered the possibility that the drug was a deadly poison...

Yet she had worn the drug on her lips. She had to have some immunity, unless she was suppressing the same hallucinations he was battling, yet he began to doubt that even a hardened assassin would place a *killing* venom on their mouth! And with this return of deductive reasoning, his will strengthened. Even if he was wrong, he still had his mind! He was able to gaze into the face of the monster, and he wasn't afraid.

"No man can resist me, Jim Anthony!" she was howling, and in her hand—in the reality Jim could now clearly see—was that tiny pistol she'd bragged about. He couldn't accurately measure distance with his altered eyesight, but he had his training. A kick upward knocked the gun away. She gave an angry cry before tackling him, but once she had made contact Jim could fight her blind. He knew every pressure point, every soft spot where the human body could be disabled. Even if her form was constantly shifting into any number of monsters—enormous apes, decrepit ghouls, even the fish-monster itself—he could feel her punching arms and kicking legs. Her nails were slicing more of the drug into his blood, but he couldn't let that stop him!

She had training too, and she slammed his head sharply against the floor of the plane. Jim tasted blood in his mouth, which he spat out harshly—he was staggered for only a few seconds and yet that was an opening he couldn't afford. She had the gun again, and leveled it against his head. Her hair was made of flames, and she had a third eye on her forehead that blazed red with hatred.

"Say *au revoir*, Super-Detective!"

But then another voice: "Jim, look out!"

Tom Gentry—looking surprisingly normal—tumbled into the brawl just as Travers pulled the trigger. Still weakened, his blow was clumsy, and yet it made all the difference in the world. Her arm snapped towards her torso, and she gave a final scream as the bullet ripped through her shoulder. Though it was a cry mostly of pain, it still had the impassioned rage that marked her savage assault on Jim Anthony.

She collapsed to the floor just as Tom helped Jim to his feet. Tom could see the pain in Jim's eyes from the beating and from the drug. Below them, Travers snarled, "This time the shot *didn't* miss the artery! *Help me*, you idiot!"

"Y-you've doomed yourself, Travers," Jim said weakly. "What I see of you is an illusion. I can't see the real you—I couldn't patch the wound even if I tried. When will the drug wear off?"

Even with the delusions, Jim could see (indeed almost *feel*) the color drain from Travers' face. "It—it won't stop for another hour."

"By which point you will be dead. I'm sorry, Margaret Travers." And he truly was.

He could hear the sound of sobbing. "God *damn* that Baron Sturm! He promised me this would be an easy job..."

"You can get your revenge on him, miss, if you tell us what he's up to," Tom Gentry interjected.

She pondered his offer for a few moments. "I don't have anything to lose," she sighed at last.

"Then what is his motive?" asked Jim.

"He...he doesn't have one."

Now it was Jim's turn to go pale. "What do you mean?"

"He killed all those people...for fun. He's a sick, deranged maniac!"

"There—has to be some slight reason, though..."

"Not in what he told me, and he told me little. A lot of it was guesswork—those crazed giggles when I was his only audience—and those *eyes*. Those evil yellow orbs...I can't imagine what the drug is making you see in me at such a high dose, but *God*, those eyes, when we were in private, they were more terrifying than any hallucination." And her voice started shaking more, and not merely from the blood loss. "He's killed many people for his own pleasure. But I took the job. It would let me retire—offered me millions. Spares no expense—he even built that tunnel from his castle to the ocean. Don't know where the money could have come from. Building it would have bankrupted even him. He had to have killed the laborers to keep them quiet. And whoever was in the suit for him that night died too—he doesn't even kill in person sometimes, he just enjoys hearing the screams...

"All I had to do was wait on a beach after your probe went through the tunnel. The thugs he hired picked it up to trap you, but he figured you'd beat them. He's a paranoiac, prepared for anything. I was to give you another dose of the drug, earn your trust, and then keep drugging you until you were helpless.

"He views you as his prize kill. Plus, if he eliminates you, there's barely anyone short of an army who can stop him from just going on killing for the rest of his life..."

Her voice broke, and her breathing became erratic. "That's all I know. I hope you destroy him. Even if I hope you die as well. I-I'm sorry I served such an evil...I don't say that to apologize to you..."

"Travers," Jim said then. "There's a spark of good in you. Die happy knowing of it. And know that *I* apologize to you."

He couldn't tell what her face looked like when she breathed her last.

At Jim's behest, Tom got a blanket from storage, and wrapped her body

"No one can resist me, Jim Anthony!"

in it before placing her somewhere secure. "When we're done with the Baron," Jim declared. "We'll find her family, and make sure she gets a proper burial."

Tom Gentry said nothing. The nobility of Jim Anthony always impressed him. But he was now equally impressed with the dead woman at his feet. She had tried to kill them for money, it was true, but the feats she must have gone through to become a match for Anthony were truly incredible. And she had nearly gotten both of them. To the last, she recognized the evil of her employer, and saw him only as a path to quitting her line of work. At heart, Tom thought, or liked to think, she was not a natural killer, but someone forced into those circumstances for some reason or another.

Now her story would never be told.

• • •

The two adventurers had a conversation while waiting for the drug to leave Jim's system. Tom recognized at once from the feelings he saw in his friend's eyes that talking about Travers wouldn't help him any. He didn't even want to commend Jim for fighting her off when he still had that hole in his leg—in any case; he was doing a better job of patching himself up. Pain was now finally flooding his body. He was hesitant to use painkillers in case they reacted with the drug (which he realized, almost as an aside, was possibly akin to that of the "control snapdragon" he'd encountered when facing the Flame Wizard, which similarly induced suggestibility), but his mother and grandfather had taught him the true meaning of strength. Pain could be suppressed. Such a thing had been necessary for their family to live on the Great Plains. And the flippancy of his father (which was only a mask over his deeper valor) had inspired an attitude that let him resist giving in to suffering, at almost any cost.

Instead they talked of the Baron Sturm. They had reason to doubt Travers' final words, but this was one time when they could ignore reason. Yet in return they tried to apply logic to the Baron, despite what the mercenary had said, though they found swiftly that there were too many possibilities. Tom put forth the theory that Sturm had been driven mad from an experience during the Great War. Only the Baron could answer, and naturally it wasn't something he seemed keen to touch on.

"What's the next step, then?" Tom asked.

"Well, if you're in a condition to fly, we need to get back to Arizona. One way or another, I think Sturm is waiting for us."

"Think he's still in police custody?"

"With Arn Benjamin on his side, probably not. It hasn't been long, but it's been long enough for he and any cohorts he may have to find a reason to let him out—I should've realized that earlier, but that first dose scrambled my wits."

Nothing else needed to be said. The *Thunderbird* took off once more, and it was a silent flight within the plane. Jim Anthony allowed himself to meditate, both on the recent events and things yet to come. The past was simple, because it could not be changed; and the future was also simple, because there was only one thing left to do. He had to stop Baron Sturm by any means necessary. Death was not the answer—at least not the first answer. It would be better to try to take him alive to face society's justice. And yet Sturm was irredeemable. His insanity was unfortunate as all madness was, but it was not an excuse for his crimes. Not when he had gone so far.

Once he felt his mind was clear, he joined Tom at the controls. He wanted to radio ahead to the Kingman Chief of Police, to ask if the Baron was still among them. He knew that he had to watch his words in case there were more traitors—but it was an innocent enough question. "*Thunderbird* to Kingman, Arizona. This is Jim Anthony to Kingman, Arizona. Over."

There was a brief pause. "We can hear you, Mr. Anthony. This is the Kingman Police Chief. Over."

"We're returning to the area. Is Baron Sturm still in your custody? Over."

"No, I'm afraid not. We discharged him almost an hour ago. One of our officers interrogated him and determined there are presently no links between him and the crime. By his permission, however, Officer Benjamin is stationed at his Castle to keep watch over the scene and maintain house arrest. More officers will be kept there at a future point as needed. Over."

Jim was silent for a few seconds, before going on: "Thank you very much. I'll give updates on my discoveries when I can. Over and out."

The Chief may have protested this abrupt cessation but Jim switched the radio off.

"If the Baron's in the Castle, Jim, he has the home advantage," the pilot said grimly. "Not to mention that even you didn't see that drug coming."

"I'm ready this time. If they do drug me again, I know I can fight with it in my system. That 'monster' is just a man in a suit, with the victims' minds doing most of the work." And he grinned, glancing at Tom's face. "And most importantly, I'm not afraid."

"Didn't think you would be, my friend," Tom Gentry said, similarly smiling.

Jim took a seat beside the pilot, and for a moment enjoyed the silence.

They landed again in Arizona, and without anything left to do to prepare, they began their journey to Castle Sturm.

• • •

This time, lacking a police escort and not wanting to call for one, the two crime-fighters were able to find a place to land the *Thunderbird* within close distance of the Castle. The drawbridge had been pulled up, of course, but among the equipment they'd taken from the plane with them was a sniper rifle. Jim Anthony didn't use such weapons on a regular basis, but they made handy tools for instances like this. He was a crack shot and so the high-caliber bullets made short work of the chains suspending the bridge. With a deafening crash the bridge came down, the wooden planks splintering and yet holding together. They then sprinted up the ramp and followed into the Castle proper.

That there would be traps was a given, but in Jim Anthony's line of work he rarely met the same trap twice. It was a fact of life he'd learned to accept that the foes he faced usually had two basic tactics of fighting him—the intellectual approach and the brute-force approach. In either case there were nearly infinite opportunities for devious originality. Any number of specialized gangs could be used in the second method, but the first showed him endlessly that there was no shortage to the combination of weapons and perils in the possession of those smart enough, rich enough, and sadistic enough. For the Baron, they were his amusement, his great game. Indeed the use of evil as a tool for passing the time seemed to be a commonality these days! And that made evil all the more meaningless.

But evil was meant to forever be sans meaning—good deeds created the world more definitively.

Jim Anthony wasn't thinking of any of this, not consciously at least. Once he and Tom were in the Castle, they saw a single police car, which likely belonged to Arn Benjamin. Aside from that the lot was empty. The Baron's fortress was large enough to conceal an army, however, if such a thing suited the needs of its master. Once they bypassed the parking area, they were confronted with the Grand Staircase. The outer set of steps led up to higher floors, while the stairs tucked between them led down to the lake chamber. Or formerly did—Jim saw with amazement that the Baron had decided to dynamite the passage! The lake was sealed away forever under a mountain of stone; evidently, he'd wanted to seal off his hidden cave with something more dramatic than the fire-door. The stairs leading up were thus only connected to the entrance by a thin strip of stone that they'd have to strafe along.

Jim hadn't had a chance to properly examine the Castle the first time he'd been here, he realized as he climbed. And so the eeriness of the place struck him for the first time. Though the areas intended for visitors, like the parking area and the lake chamber, were lit with electricity (the Baron must have had a private dynamo to keep power flowing this far out in the desert), the more private sections were lit only by candles. The orange light flickered weirdly in the stony gloom, which was a design feature— the entire thing, and not the lake cavern, was meant to resemble some Cyclopean underground temple rather than a place of habitation. Once again, theatrics were on display.

Tom's voice broke the detective's observations. "Be careful sidling this. It's basically shattered, too. Too much weight, and..." And even as he spoke, the stone gave under him! Jim risked his own balance to lash a hand out to his friend, but Tom turned it away. "I've got a handhold on the wall! Almost there..." Just another step and he made it.

Jim took the speedy approach—dancing across the ledge before it could catch his weight. This made his feet strike downward with enough force to jar loose the lip of rock, but he made it all the same. Tom was already probing the room ahead when Jim joined him. It appeared to be large rectangular room, with almost nothing in it save the candles that lit it—which tripped off Jim's sixth sense at once. Danger was afoot.

Or was it? A casual inspection of the room revealed nothing, but as they neared a doorway opposite to the entrance...

WHOOSH. The floor opened below them, like the doors of a gateway to a great walled city! Tom Gentry cried out in surprise, and just as his hands thrust to the sky to seize Jim Anthony's ankles, the sleuth's hands clambered for anything to grab in turn. Fortunately there was still just a little bit of a rim left in front of the door they'd moved towards. The fall wouldn't have been a long one, but the seasoned nostrils of the detective smelled gas—even as his eyes caught a glimpse of the new floor of the room. It was lined with a series of enormous nozzles. Just as he recognized what was going on, he heard the familiar sound of a striker—and the space below them became a mass of Dante-esque flames!

The room was filled with the sound of a sinister chuckle, broadcast over loudspeakers. "So you've figured it all out, my friends!" a Bavarian-accented voice proclaimed.

"It's Sturm!" Tom cried, his muscles bulging as he clung to Jim—as if it needed saying.

"If you want to reach me, you'll have to face a series of trials," the nobleman's voice intoned. "In addition to the ones I've set you to thus far, of course! This is the easier one—and of course the next one will be harder, and the third, harder than that! The fourth skill-test will be a duel with me. To the death, as you may expect. Because you are at the easiest stage, I will grant you a small mercy. But it has its fine print, of course!" And with another snicker at the heroes' expense, the Baron's voice stopped.

On cue, the ceiling opened in the same manner as the floor, and two ropes descended. Once they had come down, however, the lip Jim was clinging to began to recede into the wall. The ropes were within reach of the two of them—Jim obviously allowed Tom to seize one first, and with sweat on his brow the pilot climbed to escape the rising heat of the flames. Jim followed suit as soon as he was able, without a spare second to lose.

"We can use these to swing to the doorway!" Jim announced. "It's like a swing-set, Tom! Pump your legs!"

As they did so in unison, both silently wondered how this was meant to be a challenge—the flames weren't rising, even if the heat was a small agony. But once again Jim's sense of smell was his ally, as it caught another danger before his eyes did. The ropes were burning, but not from the flames—the smell, and the smoke that accompanied it, was from above! The heat was blurring the air, yet still Jim could see the source of the combustion of the ropes. Tiny droplets of clear fluid were eating away at the fibers. *Acid!*

"Pump faster, Tom! Your life depends on it!" Jim hollered. Both had a sturdy swing now, but there was no guarantee that even their strength, their adamant training, could save them now! To both of them, the flames seem to grow brighter and brighter, as if they were alive and hungry for the flesh of the morsels swinging like butcher's meat on a hook above them.

Jim was closer to the door, and so at last when he had enough swing he made a mad jump for the escape route. He'd never been so happy to feel solid ground under his feet. He spun around and saw, to his horror, that Tom wouldn't be able to make it to the doorway with the momentum he had now. But he had to try—his rope was burnt almost all the way through!

"Jump, Tom! *Jump!!*"

Tom may have lacked faith in his own abilities at that moment, but he trusted Jim Anthony. And so when he lunged and came up short, the hands of the detective were ready to take his. Jim grunted upon receiving the great muscular weight of the Irish pilot, but did not lose his footing. With his body crying out for release, Jim pulled him into the passage—and both of them were safe at last!

Jim's ally had to lean heavily against the frame of the doorway to catch his breath, while Jim watched the ropes silently split from their origin point and fall, to be roasted to ashes by the fatal pit of fire.

There was no time for further hesitation, however—especially since now Jim could hear footfalls enter the room they'd reached. They were the footsteps of a runner, and as the echoes caught up to him Jim spun with a *savate* kick he'd picked up in Paris. Through the twirl blurred his vision, he could deduce the figure's identity sure enough—it was Arn Benjamin. In his hands were two enormous meat-cleavers, and on his face was a wicked smile.

"The Baron promises an even *larger* bonus if I cut you down to size with these!" he said. "He wants to see you in chunks."

"Keep going, Jim!" Tom cried. "I'll take this muttonhead, this...this... two-bit turncoat!"

"You've got the fight in you, Tom! He's all yours!"

And Tom Gentry grinned as he spat into his fists.

Anthony went on ahead. All three of the trap chambers thus far were identical, save for the hinges on the floor or ceiling. In this room, however, was a sight that was a final assault on his senses—after seeing the fish-monster for the first time, as well as the nightmares unleashed by Sturm's hallucination-drug, there was still more to come. Hunched in the corner of the room was a humanoid figure—but one straight out of a certain novel by Victor Hugo. The figure was shirtless, and indeed would have been hard pressed to find a shirt that would fit him. Either the enormous and painful-looking bumps that covered his body were tumors of some kind, or perhaps signs of a disfigured skeleton. When he turned to face Anthony, it was with a face scarred by deep fissures that criss-crossed more lumps. The face was barely visible as the flesh was bulged out and twisted by these ghastly distortions. But the mouth was wide open, and in a sea of frothy drool could be seen yellowed teeth filed to points. In his hand was an enormous pike, yet he wielded it almost effortlessly in a single hand. He was a genuine behemoth, his greasy unkempt hair brushing against the nearly twelve-foot-high ceiling of the chamber.

"What in hell have you come up with here, Sturm?!" Anthony yelled, unable to hold back the words.

Evidently there was a hidden microphone somewhere, as the loud-speaker turned on again. "What in Hell indeed, Anthony. Was this giant of a man—I call him Morgo, by the way—born this way? Or did he end up with such an appearance from some concoction I created on the path to my dream-drug? Or perhaps he is and never was a human being?"

Anthony didn't let the Baron's words get to him. The groaning hulk was another obstacle in his quest. From the groans, he was able to deduce that he was somewhat mindless—which made him yet another victim of his enemy. He didn't want to fight the gargantuan, but it seemed he would have no choice. What he could do was make it as painless as possible, and so with a vault towards him, Anthony slammed one of his strongest blows into the giant's face.

"*RUH*—!" The bellow of the deformed unfortunate shook the very stone of the chamber. Anthony could not read his face due to the blemishes that covered it, but with his empathy sensed perhaps a pang of sadness in his opponent. The blow had forced him back and caused him to drop his pike—and in return, he raised a fist. With startling speed, he gave another cry, this one of great rage, and slammed this fist into Jim. It was a blow that would have crippled an ordinary man—the detective's brunet skin was only left covered in bruises, though he thought he felt a rib or two snap. And the giant was upon the pike again, readying to charge!

Despite losing his wind from the staggering punch, Jim was able to evade the ensuing onslaught, only to be impressed as the sharpness of the pike—or perhaps the raw power of the one wielding it—embedded the weapon several inches into the wall. A wise strategist, he knew, would understand when to abandon a fight, and when faced with a superhuman foe such as this...there was genuinely no choice.

The sleuth made for the exit while the grunting goliath struggled to pull his weapon from the wall. But once again, his breath was drawn from him as he saw what was waiting. The way to Baron Sturm's hiding place was by way of a spiral staircase, which was garnished with an almost tawdry red velvet carpet. It was the nature of this staircase, however, which boggled his mind. The steps emerged from an imposing central pillar. The pillar and its stairs were in the center of an enormous cone—there were no support rails, so if one fell, one would simply slide back to the bottom. That was—*if* they survived the fall.

It was like something out of that picture he had seen once at a repeat showing when he'd had time to drop in on one of the New York cinemas. A German film—about that mad doctor and the somnambulist he hypnotized into killing.

The pause the staircase gave him was only a brief one. He began his long and treacherous sprint even as he heard Morgo—as the Baron had called him—begin his hunt for Anthony anew. The titan screamed as his long stride put him right behind the detective. The air filled with the wretched sound—and worse scent—of his labored breathing. Anthony craned his head upward and battled off despair as he saw how high the stairs reached.

But all torments end, one way or another, and before he knew it, Jim Anthony had passed through another threshold—and a now-familiar voice called out, "Morgo, halt."

Morgo obeyed the command, but Jim's tension did not fade. He was now in the exotic office of the Baron Sturm.

· · ·

The Baron's seeming insistence on electricity supplying only a minority of the Castle's light continued into how he set up the trappings of his office. The room, which would have been cozy in other circumstances, was lit by only three candles, which were mounted on the ancient mahogany desk Sturm had posed himself on. There was a bookshelf on Jim's left that had the sort of moldy volumes that also seemed to be from one of the popular horror pictures—but Jim was able to tell, even at a distance, that many of these books were fake. He had no doubt that somewhere else in the Castle was a grand library with the sort of tomes best read at midnight during thunderstorms, and that these false volumes were merely to add to the Universal Pictures atmosphere. Completing it all was a moldy green rug that stood in deliberate contrast to the crimson carpet of the stairs.

It was Jim Anthony's first time seeing Sturm in person. He definitely fit the part, though Jim was at a loss as to what actor he resembled. The mustache was very much of the Old World, it was true, and the balding scalp revealed an age that touched another century, but even the most shocking of film stars, or the most infamous of 19th Century faces, lacked the penetrating golden eyes of his enemy. Anthony would have tried to make one last judgment of the Baron's character based on his attire, but he had already seen it before—albeit in an illusion. He was clad in the sapphire-scaled garb of the fish-humanoid! Only the mask remained off, and it sat beside him on the desk.

"I'd welcome you, Mr. Anthony, if I hadn't technically done so already," smiled the wicked Baron.

"And I ran out of curses to throw at you on the jog up the stairs, Baron Sturm," the crime-fighter replied.

"I don't mean to talk for awhile. I want to get to killing you as quick as possible. But before I do so, I have to satisfy a craving of mine, one which you seem to already be familiar with in me. Morgo, please come here."

The colossus made no sound as he sidestepped around Anthony, approaching the Baron. The latter man held his hands out, and Morgo gave him the pike. Jim's eyes widened as he realized what was happening, but before he could cry out, "No! *Don't!!*" the Bavarian impaled Morgo through the belly. There was a final groan of pain, mixed with a muted question, a final wordless "Why?" Blood spattered over the shaft of the pike and onto the blue roughness of the monster costume. Morgo collapsed and his body met its resting place crumpled in the office's corner.

And suddenly, Sturm began giggling in the fashion that must have brought chills to Margaret Travers. It was a long string of small connected giggles that went on and on until the nobleman had tears in his eyes. Then suddenly those eyes locked onto those of Jim Anthony.

"That made up for things. There's been a lapse since I've had a chance to do it in person. As wonderful as the last party was—I wish I had been in the costume that evening."

"In the name of...whatever you worship, Baron—why?!"

"I could tell you why," the Baron hissed through the teeth of his smile. "But I can't guarantee it would be true."

"Tell me anyway."

"Perhaps as a child I was shown a copy of Plato's *Timaeus*, and I let its story of Atlantis run away with me. Perhaps I later discovered the modern theories about the Lost Continent—like those of Madame Blavatsky—and it opened my eyes to the possibilities of this world. In fact, it's possible that the Atlanteans, with their theorized mastery of science, and of the mysterious *vril* force of Bulwer-Lytton, allowed them to survive their descent into the depths. But the resultant creatures, the products of adaptation, were no longer what they once were...as inhuman as you must imagine me to be."

Anthony didn't hide the skepticism in his face, even when it appeared to bring continued amusement to the Baron.

"These creatures are, of course, from my own imagination—even Blavatsky leaves no record of them. But it's possible—just possible—that this story was enough for me to dedicate my life to usurping the legacy of Atlantis—by becoming one of the fabled fish-men!" He waited for a second, and then burst out laughing. "No, detective, that is not the truth. Plato created the story of Atlantis as a metaphor. It was not real. But that was not to say that there couldn't be *some* ancient lost lands, somewhere, to begin with. Perhaps with *real* monsters, eh? Ones even worse than poor dead Morgo.

"But now is not the time to discuss such things. The truth is that I simply enjoy killing. I like taking a life, something complicated and beautiful, and crushing it in my hands, or tearing its throat out. It is my way of spitting in the Eye of the Creator, though that too is an over-complication of my, er, what do you call it? *Modus operandi?*"

"That is the term, yes."

The Baron donned the hideous scaly mask that completed his outfit. The weight of all of it didn't seem to bother him, for the strength of mania churned within him.

"I suppose we fight now. I warn you, Jim Anthony—nobility has not softened me. And this suit has a few tricks to it."

And abruptly, he unleashed a monstrous howl that would curdle the blood of most. With an astonishing quickness, he sprinted towards Anthony, and the duel to the death began!

Typically when two combatants are master fighters—by merit of training or sheer ferocity—the battle is over quickly. And so it was when the Baron got his hands on his enemy. Anthony once again suppressed a syllable of surprise, for he discovered right away that the scales of suit were covered in infinitesimally small barbs that left minute but painful slashes across his torso, ripping through his shirt and scratching the palms he raised in self-defense. Beneath the mask Jim could hear the Baron's signature laugh, which lapsed seemingly at random between the private giggle and chuckle from the loudspeakers. The chuckle must have been to spare the giggle—the giggle was to be saved when the Baron's foes were close to the heart of his madness.

Sturm was easily able to shove Anthony out of the office and back onto the precarious staircase. Jim tried to pull away, but in vain. All the same he was a man of improvisation, and by this point he'd assessed that his enemy's strength was also his weakness. If he was stuck to Sturm, Sturm was also stuck to him. With this in mind, he braced himself for the pain, and imitated the throw he had used on Sturm's hired gun in Frisco.

He didn't know if tossing the Baron would rip the skin from his palms or if they would remain stuck together through the barbs. It turned out to be the latter, and though he tried to keep his balance and remain on the stairs, it was an impossible feat. Both of the men gawkily plunged from the staircase into a free-fall, with only the sloped walls of the conical structure to stop them. But because of how Jim had thrown the Baron, the nobleman would take the impact. The detective still felt it when they hit, yet the suit protected Sturm—the contact would have broken his spine otherwise. They slid down the bottom of the enormous chamber, and still, the barbs bit into Jim's flesh.

The sly Baron managed to land on his feet, and before Anthony could react he kicked into his chest. *That* leverage was enough to jar forth the barbs, and as Anthony had anticipated—all the flesh on his palms was ripped away. The pain shook even him, though again he didn't take notice of the pain. Once again, Sturm was too fast, and his desire to get to his favorite part of a brawl was strong. The webbed gloves were on Jim's neck, and the Baron forced him to his knees.

For a moment it looked like it was already over. The sharp pain now surrounding Jim's throat was a harbinger for his impending death. He didn't know what awaited him on the other side. Perhaps for his life as a warrior, the spirits of his tribe would reward him. Or maybe his Irish side would determine his fate, and he would be judged for Heaven or Hell. He only regretted now, in this direst time, that he had not said something more profound at the end to his grandfather Mephito, to Tom Gentry, to his friends at the *New York Star* or the fighting girls of Maria Flores. To any of the people who had risked their safety and sanity to aid him in his life...

But his eyes caught something—a figure, staggering weakly at the top of the spiral staircase. It was the freakish Morgo, who was pale from loss of blood. In his mighty hand was the pike that had been his undoing. He was holding it high, with the tip facing down—and then he dropped it.

With a newfound strength, the Irish-Comanche lost more skin escaping the grip of the insane Baron, whose giggle had grown a thousand times louder in the echoes of the chamber, and as Jim's ears strained hard when he was so close to death. As if by a danger sense such as Jim's own, Baron Sturm looked up—but unlike Jim's, his sense had kicked in far too late.

A sick, wet impact resounded through the cone. And with a death rattle, Sturm, and the fish-creature he'd created in himself, were mercilessly struck from the Earth.

• • •

It had been a humbling adventure.

Jim Anthony had needed his chauffeur's help in climbing the stairs to see if anything could be done for the massive Morgo. But as with Margaret Travers, the circumstances prevented any aid from coming. Jim was tempted to chastise Tom when he had a nauseous reaction to seeing the dead man's deformities, but he lacked the energy. As with Travers, however, he would ensure that this minion of the Baron Sturm would get a proper burial.

Tom Gentry had defeated the rogue policeman in hand-to-hand combat, as Jim had expected him to. Benjamin was now securely bound with the pilot's belt.

By inspecting Sturm's office, they'd found a secret passage that let them at last leave the monstrous Castle. They'd also found the listening mechanisms through which Sturm monitored his "guests," even though that mattered less.

It was becoming twilight when they silently rested in the Arizona sands. They did have to rest before returning to the *Thunderbird*, to let the police know it was all over. To say anything now would be almost sacrilegiously awkward. But in time, Tom Gentry had to say something, because he saw the deep pain in his friend's face.

"What's on your mind?" the pilot asked.

Jim was upfront about it, as the desire to maintain silence had started to wane in him. "Weirdly enough, out of all the people who died as a result of that lunatic...Travers. Travers is who I'm thinking about. I wasn't lying when I said I saw that spark of good in her—even if she made a lifestyle out of ending people's lives."

"That's another woman that tricked you by passing as someone she wasn't," Tom said bitterly. "After Ms. Somerset, you know. You really gotta watch out for them. Or settle down someday, maybe? Let a wife come do this stuff with us and you'll have an excuse to avoid the ladies."

Anthony continued staring out. "It's not the sex I'm distrusting, Tom. Women are clearly capable agents in our enemy's hands, just as men are. But it's more important—in the end—to see how indispensable their vast skills are to do good."

Tom caught a note that he didn't like in Anthony's voice. "You're talking like...with Travers and with Somerset...there's one enemy? One linking the both of them?"

Anthony just watched the sun come down, descending from far up in the sky.

End of Part Two

"What's on your mind?"

VOYAGE OF CRIME

The butler Dawkins never rested when his master was in the Penthouse. Of course, he didn't rest when his master was away from it, either. But for the first time since he'd started this job, he was lying exhausted on a couch, and with good reason. He had just suffered the beating of his life!

The small Cockney man was resting in the expansive suite that topped one of the most impressive skyscrapers in Manhattan. A significantly larger man was crouched at his side, trying to dab blood off of his forehead. Dawkins moaned in pain, but Tom Gentry's voice tried to sooth him. Behind them, bare-footed, standing tall, and with hands behind his back, was Dawkins' employer, the brunet-skinned world-famous detective Jim Anthony.

He was staring out the window at the city below. The Waldorf-Anthony building towered above much of the rest of the metropolis, and thus the dark eyes of the Irish-Comanche swept over it all with an uncanny precision. His motivation was inscrutable. Perhaps he was searching for the man who had attacked his butler—or maybe he was simply debating what his strategy would be for tracking down the assailant. This sort of intense seriousness would come over the crime-fighter at times and when it did, there was a certain chill in the room. Even if the military-grade radiators were keeping them warm against the cold of 1937's November.

Jim and Tom had already interrogated Dawkins when Waldorf-Anthony security had brought him to the Penthouse, but he was too weak to say much. "'E was crazy, sah," was all he had gotten out. "Utterly, totally crazy..." And then the bloody wound on his head caught up with him. All told, he had a bruised skull, three cracked ribs, and two broken arms, plus other small abrasions all over his body. It was obvious that the butler's description of his attacker was right—this was the work of an absolute madman!

It had been almost eight hours since Dawkins had passed out, and while Jim had wanted to give him a chance to recover, the trail was growing cold with every passing minute. He spoke the first words he'd given since he'd examined his servant. "Let's try to wake him up, Tom. There are more painkillers in the medicine cabinet when he comes to."

"I'm on it," Tom Gentry replied. The cabinet in question was mounted high up next to the doorway to the focal point of the Penthouse—the unequaled laboratory from which Jim Anthony would sometimes conduct his cutting-edge experiments. He had many such facilities all over the world, but the Penthouse was one of his fortresses, a place that made him feel truly safe and secure.

But as the pilot reached for the medicine cabinet, he did so in a way that stretched his shoulder. This shoulder had been the subject of a gunshot wound just a few days prior—the hired gun Margaret Travers had injured Tom before her accidental death. Tom was a powerful man, but he flinched and gasped as pain flooded half his body. When he turned, he was caught off-guard by the fact that Jim was already standing next to him, his face struggling to mask his concern.

"I'm sorry, Tom—I forgot," the detective said. "Maybe you should rest, too. You were exhausted during the last case anyway...the additional circumstances the case brought didn't help much."

"Jim, I'm fine..."

"Tom. I'm giving an *order* to rest. I want you to stay at the Penthouse. If I need to go anywhere for this case—if it actually goes anywhere—I can always take the auto-gyro."

Tom said nothing. As an assistant of Jim Anthony, he wasn't about to disobey a direct order. But as Jim's oldest friend and closest confidant, he was slightly stung. It was true, yes, that his wound was still recent enough to be called "fresh." And it was true, he hadn't had much relief from physical exhaustion recently. Tending to Dawkins had gone late into the night, and both he and Jim had been awake now for more than twenty-four hours. But considering this made Tom realize that his desire to support his friend had been the only motivator keeping him awake—he had desperately craved sleep but forced himself to ignore the urge. Though he would sleep uneasily, knowing that soon Jim was about to hit the streets to search for the crazy fool who had attacked Dawkins, he would be able to accept his orders on both a personal and professional level.

Shortly, as Jim was ready to wake up the butler, Tom Gentry was setting up a cot in the lab. He'd rest all through the next day.

Dawkins rose uneasily. "Where am I...?" he asked, his vision muddled before him.

"In the Penthouse, Dawkins. Don't worry, it's me. Take these."

After the butler swallowed the pills with water, he seemed more at ease. "It was 'orrible, Mawster Anthony—an' I don't think too many things are 'orrible these days. Blimey! I was just out to get the milk, yes? And suddenly, this nutter comes up to me, staggerin' like somethin' out of that zombie movie with the Lugosi fellow."

"What did he look like, Dawkins?" Jim asked.

The valet paused for a few moments. "Can't say I remember, sah. I'm right sorry, I am. It must be the knock on the noggin..."

"I understand, Dawkins. But try to remember."

The butler squeezed his eyes shut. "I-I think I'll have a better picture in a few moments, sah."

Jim waited patiently at Dawkins' side, as the latter had waited with similar stony calm at his side all these years. But in his mind, there was great concern over the events that had taken place. In his life, minor incidents such as these often had as much of a ripple effect as the shocking, unbelievable crimes he often assigned himself to. Dawkins was certainly no pushover—as one of Jim's employees and allies he received some of the best self-defense training in the world. If only he could speak more of the incident, then he'd have deeper insight into the situation! But he hadn't wanted to leave his faithful servant's side—and his own medical care often exceeded what a hospital could give.

Overshadowing the concern of crime was Jim's worry about what his line of work was doing to his friends and associates. Tom would be out of action for awhile, and he wanted Dawkins to stay safe until he healed up. And yet if his worries about crime were justified, his concerns over his friends would have to wait. Love was always sacrificed for justice in the world of Jim Anthony. But the circumstances meant he was down two assistants. He had many confederates all around the world, and yet Dawkins and Tom Gentry were among the friends he interacted with the most—besides his grandfather Mephito, of course. He would have to think hard to select the next operative to aid him, if it came down to that.

His line of thought was interrupted by the phone blaring loudly. Jim went to go answer.

"Jim Anthony speaking."

"Anthony, this is the NYPD. We have an assault case on our hands that seems completely irregular."

"How so?" He considered letting the man on the other end know he was possibly about to get wrapped up in an assault incident of his own.

"I'll describe in person. We have the suspect in custody at Headquarters. Please come at once, if you can."

"I'll be over as soon as possible."

Like Tom Gentry, Jim couldn't resist a summons to action. Dawkins' injuries weren't going to get any worse, and though he was sleeping, Tom was on hand to help with anything that could come up.

"Dawkins," the detective said hurriedly. "I'm going to check out a police matter, but I'll return soon."

"Tan," the butler said in response.

Jim briefly halted. "What was that?"

"'E 'ad a very unseasonable tan, sah, for November."

The detective put a finger to his lips in contemplation. But thoughts would have to wait. For now, the police were waiting.

• • •

An officer by the name of Collins was escorting Jim Anthony through the halls of the Headquarters of the New York Police Department. He'd explained on the way in that he was taking him to see the suspect immediately. "The Chief doesn't want to waste any time," he stated.

Jim asked, "What's the hurry?"

"I don't know myself, Mr. Anthony. The Chief's been addled lately. The President has assigned departments throughout the country to pool resources and try to figure out missing persons cases. Pretty unusual. Breaks the Chief's sense of organization, I think."

"And what's the deal with these missing persons?"

"A couple of cruise ships vanished off the West Coast. There can't be any sort of connection between this and that, though."

Jim Anthony was not so sure. Crimes were often like spiderwebs, with many threads stretching out everywhere. Just as spiders removed insect pests from the world, however, Jim Anthony freed the world of the spiders who spun these webs.

But he still lacked vital details. In many ways he hoped this case was not related to any others on his mind: the one Collins had mentioned, and the one concerning his butler Dawkins. He wanted to wrap up what lay ahead quickly so he could return to the latter case in particular.

Yet when he was taken to the holding cell, his hopes for such simplicity vanished. The man sitting on the bed within the cell had an odd color to his skin. A very unseasonable tan.

Aside from that, there was another detail which struck the detective right away: his face was the look of epitomized trauma. His eyes stared forward blankly, unblinking, beneath a carroty patch of balding hair. His face was full of an agonized and unending tension, as if having been injected with a paralytic. Indeed, Anthony could tell that this tension flooded his whole body, and the pain of this tension had caused him to break out in a thick sweat.

"Hard to tell what sort of lunatic he is," Officer Collins. "Most of the ones I've met have screamed and thrown things when they've been locked up. He seems pretty okay with the whole deal."

"His will's been broken somehow," Jim Anthony said then. "This is a shell of a man. Only way this could have happened is through torture or... drugs." To Collins, Anthony's face seemed to flicker with some sort of emotion, but it was too slight a motion to make sense of. "I don't suppose interrogation helped?"

"Actually, Mr. Anthony, it's the other way around. He was ready to talk. He'd tell us anything—but the problem is he won't specify."

"Or can't. Let me try."

Jim approached the cell. "Excuse me, sir. I just want to ask you a few questions." Silence. "What is your name?"

"I have a name."

A dull, monotone voice—exactly what Jim was expecting. "What is it?"

"What is what?"

"Your name."

"I have a name."

Jim paused for a second. "Why did you attack those people?"

"He told me to defend myself."

The sleuth felt one of his eyebrows arch. He turned to look at Collins. "That's what he told us, too," the officer said.

"Who is he?" Jim asked.

"Who is who?"

"Who is the one who told you to defend yourself?"

"It was he."

"Fine. What is the *name* of the person who told you to defend yourself?"

"I do not know."

Collins stepped in again. "We didn't get *that* far. Ask what he did."

"What did the...what did the man who told you to defend yourself do to you to make you act in this way?"

"He did not do anything. It was the sea air. The bad sea air."

Jim was intrigued, and took a few steps closer to the cell. "What is the bad sea air?"

But the man was silent.

"What is the bad air?"

More silence!

"What is the plan of the one who told you to defend yourself?"

"We must all defend ourselves."

Jim Anthony was getting stumped, and it was showing. But behind him, there was the sudden sound from the radio mounted on the table behind Collins. "Collins, this is the Chief! Is Jim Anthony still down there with you? Over."

"Yes, he is!" Collins said. "What's going on? Over."

"Tell him he's needed back at the Penthouse! His chauffeur called—his headquarters is under attack!"

Jim didn't wait to hear more. "I'm going to drive back at once!" he called. "Keep him in custody!"

"Wait...! I'm coming with you!" Collins cried. As they ran back upstairs, he called out to an officer named Jenkins to guard the cell, and the entranced man within. Jim considered briefly that Collins was being impulsive, but there was no time to stop him. There was only time for action, the only salvation of Anthony's friends.

Officer Jenkins was left to guard the tanned man in the basement. Headquarters was relatively empty now—many officers were on their beats, or working on the cruise ships case with the Chief. For a few moments there was no noise, and Jenkins was reading the *New York Star* while occasionally glancing up at the suspect. Only sometimes there was the crackling as he turned the pages of the paper. It was only natural that he jumped in surprise when the radio went off behind.

A hushed voice came from the speakers. "Return to the ocean."

Jenkins turned suddenly. "Hm?"

Jenkins' radio continued to speak. "Return to the ocean," the voice whispered.

Slowly, the prisoner began to rise. Jenkins began to realize what was happening and he went to turn the radio off. But even without power, the voice continued to speak through it! "Return to the ocean, my subject," it kept saying.

The prisoner was putting his hands on the bars of his cell, and was leaning forward. Jenkins wouldn't have believed it if he couldn't see it with his own two eyes—the bars were bending under the tanned madman's hands! He was ready to call for backup, and thought he'd have time for it. But just as the steel bars snapped, the lunatic suddenly sped up, and rushed right at him! In his hand was a broken piece of pipe, which he was wielding like a club...

The police station was flooded with Jenkins' final screams.

And had there been anyone near his body when he died, they would have heard the radio continue to murmur, in a voice that grew more and more intense with a swelling hatred: "Return to the ocean. Return to the ocean! *Return to the ocean!*"

Jenkins' hands shook from the pain coursing through his body. He'd heard his skull *crack*, and he knew from that sound alone that he was a dead man.

• • •

Jim Anthony stood at the base of the Waldorf-Anthony, but he wasn't standing in place for more than a second. The elevator could get him and Collins to the Penthouse in about twenty seconds. But would that be too late to save his injured compatriots?

The employees on the entry level didn't get a chance to put the "-lo" on "Hel-." The two men were in the elevator at once, and were rocketing up to the top floor, where the pilot and valet were perhaps making a last stand. Jim was squirming with anxiety all the way up, but Collins didn't dare comment on it. He was filled with a private anxiety of his own—a desire to avoid disappointing his personal hero, with whom he now shared the elevator.

When the elevator opened Jim lunged out with both grace and urgency. And up ahead, banging on the door into the Penthouse from elevator bay, was another tanned man, who shared Jim's desire to reach the apartment but in a different manner of expression. The door was in ruins, and he was climbing in. Within the apartment, Jim could hear his radio turned on— and there was a voice coming over. "Destroy Jim Anthony and his helpers," it muttered. "Destroy Jim Anthony and his helpers."

"Tom, Dawkins! Turn the radio off!"

"Jim?! Jim, is that you—?!"

"Mawster Anthony! Thanks Heavens you've returned, sah!"

They were okay for now. The man, acting as though possessed, was indeed making his way into the room, but Jim jerked him back and threw him against the wall.

"Tom, destroy the radio—you *must* destroy it!"

Tom didn't hesitate, and seized the machine. The heavy radio hurt his shoulder but adrenaline overwhelmed the pain. "Listen to me. You must destroy Jim Anthony and his helpers. You must destroy..." Dawkins opened the window, and hurriedly Tom pitched the speaking box out.

Once it was gone—with a glance to make sure no one was hit—there was no other voice afflicting the man. Jim saw he was a different one from the one at the station, and at once his fears were confirmed. This was a large-scale crime operation. These operatives were part of a conspiracy against the United States, or at least New York. And they were almost definitely drugged, which opened up a new too-big coincidence. An enemy he fought not long ago, the Flame Wizard, used drugs to control people, made from the snapdragon *Antirrhinum imperius*. Then Baron Sturm, whom he'd faced just a few days ago, had used a hallucination-causing drug that he had used to lead Jim Anthony himself astray. Both men had clever traitorous female operatives at their disposal. Jim had suspected in the wake of both cases that one villain was behind it all, and now with another mind-control drug in play, it had to have been the same master criminal. He would have to crack this case immediately—if he didn't, these clever plots would destroy innocent lives with unchecked power.

"That's the same fellow who came for me, Mawster Anthony!" Dawkins explained.

"I'll make sure to leave instructions on how to properly contain him," Jim said. "Ordering him to...*not* escape would probably work."

Just then, from the laboratory, there was another voice. "There's the other radio, in the lab—it's still in one piece," Tom said. "I woke up awhile ago and was listening in on the police wavebands. Just before that loony showed up, the authorities were saying that their tanned prisoner was escaping!"

"Then this was a diversion—as well as a real attempt to kill the two of you and wreck our base here," Jim replied. "That man in the cell may have done something to the police station!"

He didn't have time to specify what exactly that could be. The radio speakers blew out as they broadcast the sound of a mighty explosion.

• • •

When Jim Anthony stood amidst the dancing ghosts of smoke, his expression was one of his darkest yet—and many of the seasoned officers here had seen him serious before. There was an enormous hole in the floor of the station's reception lobby, exposing the holding cells below. The first thing he had seen when he walked down the remnants of the stairs to see the damage was a charred pile of ashes that had once been a man named Harold Jenkins.

The realization that his current case was probably tied to the two that preceded it, as well as the sheer intensity of his enemy's attack this time around was at the root of the anger stemming from the detective. He kept that a secret from no one. And though his presence was usually a beacon of hope and cheer for police the world over, the obvious frustration radiating from his powerful body meant that this time, he was an emblem of fear. Even for those who dedicated themselves to justice.

"It's just good so many of us were gone," Collins said then.

"And that the explosion was so small," Jim murmured. "The bomb could've destroyed the entire station, but it must have been rather tiny itself. You didn't catch it on booking him. The villain behind it—the master villain I mentioned—wanted to scare us and show us his power, his reach, without eliminating us entirely. Which fits the men he's employed or supplied. The Flame Wizard and Baron Sturm certainly relished their thespian reveals—the *impact* of their power. Sometimes at the cost of victory."

At once Collins became aware from Jim's words that these were the sorts of cutthroats he faced on a regular basis. Great men like Anthony were oftentimes great simply by the scale of the villains they stopped. And in time, as they got a taste for facing that particular breed of darkness-dweller, or as they became famous for that fight, it would consume their life. In a world like this, Jim Anthony could never live as normal men could. For a brief moment, Collins felt almost a shade of pity for the so-called Super Detective. He had the minor shock when he realized that few people besides him had ever felt that pity.

"We'll know right away if a car catches him, however," Collins said weakly. Then, even more faintly, "He couldn't have gotten far."

"I hope so," Anthony said. But he said nothing else.

The detective's brain was filled with another source of stress—his sixth sense, which could feel danger as easily as his fingers felt the steel of a doorknob, had been buzzing almost constantly since he'd taken Dawkins in. There were peaks in its rhythm now and then, but he could not help but wonder if these continuous attacks were based on his foe's knowledge of that sense. He couldn't rule out the possibility that the repeated assaults were meant to overload his power, and thus take away the advantage it gave him. Admittedly, in the last handful of cases, it had done little to warn him simply because he was surrounded by constant danger.

But gently, he had closed his eyes and filled his lungs with fresh air. He dove deep into his own mind, to try to parse apart the various caution stimuli that defined this superhuman portion of his brain. He envisioned it like a endocardiogram, with a baseline and significant peaks. At first he could also see a narrow band of this, representing what he felt in the moment. But by concentrating, and expanding his field of vision, he could see peaks of the past, and those to come as well. And there was a big shock coming...*now*.

The radio nearby went off.

"Collins, this Car 14, are you there?"

"This is Collins. Go ahead, Car 14."

"That terrorist who escaped—we're right on his trail now."

Jim Anthony butted in then. "Where are you, Car 14?"

"Getting close to New York Harbor along Clove Street. He may be trying to get to a ship."

Jim sprinted suddenly from the radio. "Jim!" Collins cried. He too bolted, following closely on the detective's footsteps. But he was mortal, or at least less immortal than Jim. And so it was that Collins was left behind once Anthony reached his car.

He briefly cursed. For a second, he thought he was going to get to be a part of this adventure! It would've been what he really needed with this oft-boring beat—and he felt as though Jim Anthony had needed it. Again, his vision of the human dimension of Anthony flared up, and with it came that smallest hint of pity.

Yet wherever he went, Anthony would have someone to help him. Though his parents were gone, he had the biggest family in the world. Still, Collins ached over missing his chance to become a part of it!

• • •

Jim Anthony wasn't sparing any rubber on his way to New York Harbor. He had a suspicion that the assailant—now a murderer—was going to elude the police. There was a cleverer person at the puppet-strings. And it seemed as though every radio in the city could be used by the mysterious whisperer. His voice could reach his servants anywhere.

Jim was wondering about that voice. Presumably he conditioned his servants to prioritize his commands over those of others—otherwise when they attacked people, the screams of "Stop!" from their victims would work. But isolated from that controlling voice, they slowly became more suggestible to the commands of others. Or Jim and the police had spoken authoritatively enough to control them.

He was going to stop all of this now, though. No more drug-slaves for the master crook. No more murders, no more terror.

Jim saw the repeat use of narcotics as representing a chilling demand for absolute perfection. Only scapegoats, the smokescreen criminals (as Sturm and the Flame Wizard had turned out to be), were allowed to make mistakes. Everyone else was either tortured with hallucinations or had their wills broken by chemicals that emptied the subject's minds.

This villain was the Great Spider—so huge that even Anthony the spider-killer would be hard pressed to wipe him out.

There he was!

Not the master, of course, but the escaping terrorist. Sprinting with a super- (or maybe sub-) human endurance, he was already very close to the boarding plank of one of the great cruise ships taking passengers to the worlds beyond the ocean. Jim stepped on the gas and closed in even as the man tried to hide himself in the crowd. Nothing could escape the eyes of Jim Anthony, but before he could act, the man was aboard!

The car screeched to a halt and Jim burst out to spring after his prey. And yet the plank was being raised, and the ship was leaving the harbor. Not even his authority could stop the ship in time.

As he reached dock, he stopped the man who'd check the passengers. Somehow the suspect had broken past him unnoticed.

"Where is this ship heading?" the detective bellowed over the sounds of the boat's klaxons.

"Panama Canal!" the man yelled back, with an accent Jim didn't bother placing.

"Thank you!"

Jim was momentarily frozen in contemplation. Panama! There was no time to lose. He could contact the American authorities in Panama, of course. They'd be ready to catch the prisoner...and...

He was jarred out of this momentary thought by the police sirens rising behind him. NYPD Car 14 was there—far too late.

Jim explained the situation but spoke fast—almost too fast for the officers to catch properly. Then he was back in his car again. It was time to head to another harbor, or rather, a pier. He was racing to none other than his secret dock in Long Island, where the speedboat *Comanche* was docked!

• • •

The velocity of Jim's car was soon replaced with the similarly unbeatable speed of the *Comanche*. She could make about 110 knots, or nearly 130 miles per hour. Even at that rate, it would take around eleven or twelve hours to reach Panama Canal, not counting stopovers at one of the Caribbean islands to refuel (though the *Comanche* had one of the most generous gas tanks on the seas). But that was still better than the passenger ship. Jim set his course and took a seat on the deck, his legs crossed, to meditate.

The *yoga* methods changed his perception of time so it was not quite such a long voyage. And here, on the open seas, he was at last liberated from the endlessness of his sixth sense, and so once again it had meaning for him. In his trance, his sense was easier to make sense of anyway, and it would ensure the safety of his voyage even while entranced. Even the slightest risk would register to him and he would be able to snap into action. But by the time he stopped over in Haiti, he had few interruptions outside of changing course.

He was surprised that he was able to leave Haiti without incident. In the related cases, it seemed as if everywhere he could possibly go had a trap waiting. But he appreciated the continued break from his danger sense.

Within a few hours, he was in Panama.

When he pulled up to the pier, he was met with several members of the Panamanian Army. They spoke to him first in Spanish, then in English. He understood them both times. "Detenéis! Identifíquese! Stop and identify!"

He held up his hands as he approached. He was clad in his boots, jophurs and tan khaki shirt. Around his middle was a tight belt. The loop served as a belt, certainly, but it was also one of Jim Anthony's greatest tools. It was actually a rope with a weighted ball at the end, which could be used as a grapple—or a weapon. Against heights or mobs, Jim was hardly defenseless; however, in some of his more recent cases he had left this belt behind in the rush of going out. But this time things were different, even if he doubted he'd have to resort to violence here.

"Yo soy Jim Anthony," he said simply, grinning.

At first the soldiers seemed to disbelieve him, but confusion spread across their faces as he got into better light—then the confusion melted to a joyful surprise.

"Señor Anthony, it is an honor!" the one at the fore of them said. "What are you doing in Panama at this hour?"

"I've just driven the *Comanche* here from New York City. I'm tracking a criminal!"

"Your determination! Dios santo! He must be a deadly criminal indeed—and he is yet undetected in Panama—!"

"Don't worry, soldier...I don't think he's here yet. But when he arrives, I'll be waiting for him."

But he was, upon reaching land, suddenly very weary. The meditation had been unable to replace sleep. He forced himself to stay conscious, however—in his last case, exhaustion, as well as exposure to drugs, caused him to lose focus and be overcome. Since some sort of drug was probably at play here, he didn't want history to repeat itself. His success—and confidence—depended on it.

"What is your plan, then, Señor Anthony?"

"I'm going to monitor all incoming ships going into the Canal. If that ship does come here—I'll recognize it." And this time, though he did not say this aloud, he would be able to truly stop the man.

From there he could sail for the location of the vanished ships in the South Pacific. He had recorded the location thanks to one of his reporters at the *New York Star* who'd been assigned to the story.

And so he began his night-long vigil—with each second pressing hard on him. And yet he had come through his previous bout of exhaustion as a stronger man. His will would not fade him tonight, nor would it again.

• • •

The dawn was just breaking when the ship began passing through. Jim Anthony tensed his muscles and sprung into action.

First he climbed the building that served as the headquarters of the port authority. One of the officers inside, despite his experience, jumped as he saw the bronze-skinned adventurer tapping at his window. He, like the soldiers, recognized the man as Jim Anthony, once his heart slowed to a normal pace again. He opened the window.

"Señor Anthony! What can I do for you?"

"I need you to detain that ship. There is a dangerous criminal aboard that I've been tracking down from New York, and I need to place him under arrest."

"But—what about the safety of the passengers? Have you considered that?"

"The man is not dangerous by himself but can be given commands to become dangerous." And Jim took a risky pause then. "But I will move hurriedly, and if he attacks anyone I will defend them—if he tries to take hostages I will ensure that they are unharmed at any cost."

"I trust you, Señor Anthony."

"I will make sure your trust is not misplaced."

And without further ado, he bounded down the side of the building, and boarded the ship.

His eyes swept every square inch of the ship's deck, before even the passengers looking his way could see him. Where was the hypnotized killer hiding? He could be anywhere, and Jim indeed desired to keep his promise to stop the assassin quickly so as to keep the passengers safe. At first it seemed as though his search was in vain...

And yet, crouching and crab-walking behind a crowd of passengers was the distinct Pacific-tanned skin! He must have received a command—at some point—to keep himself hidden. That meant there was a chance he was being commanded now. Jim lithely made his way through the crowd of passengers, and only some of them took notice of his swift dodge between them. The man saw him coming—and bolted.

Unlike Jim, the escaping killer used brute force to get through the crowd, eliciting many cries of surprise. Jim knew it was his responsibility to stop those cries from becoming screams. But the stiffened face of the former prisoner appeared to have the vague intimations of *fear*, rather than murderous intent. Still, he was fast—he had probably slept, if such a thing were possible in his state, and thus had a leg up on Jim. He was at the edge of the deck, and he frog-leaped over the edge, clearing a surprising distance. To Jim's chagrin he had landed on top of the wall of the canal. It was a jump that Jim could mimic, certainly, but he'd already let a significant distance come between them. He was heading towards the closest city, which was not far from the port.

The tips of Jim's boots pushed off the side of the ship, and soon he, too, was sprinting towards the limits of the city of Colón. He estimated that the man was about a hundred yards away. It would be easy enough to close, if he could dodge traffic...

And yet suddenly, with a muted gasp of pain, the man dropped to the ground.

Jim was set on edge, even if his danger sense had suddenly faded. Was the man dead, or merely unconscious? It looked as though he had been shot, but by whom, and from where? Would they be gunning for Jim Anthony as well...?

But just then, a figure sprinted out towards the man's crumpled form. Her long raven hair was blowing in the wind, and she was clad in what some esoteric fashion aficionados were starting to call a cat-suit, made out of a dark composite material that Jim didn't recognize. The skintight outfit covered every inch of her—all save her neck and head, of course—but was one of the most revealing get-ups Jim had seen in awhile. Few women on Earth could match the curves of that figure. Certainly she was a most feminine woman, and yet the cat-suit, Jim knew, hid a body as muscular as his own. This particular person—for Jim was well familiar with her—had been involved with these sorts of field operations for as long as he had. He was glad to have her in his employ, though his relationship with Maria Flores was a mutually beneficial partnership rather than a petty boss-worker link.

"Señora Flores!" he called out, his voice loaded with genuine gladness.

She glanced over at him, and her face lit up, though not in surprise. "Jim Anthony! My darling!" she cried. "Why is it our paths always seem to cross here, in this city, out of all the towns in all the Americas?"

"Perhaps destiny wills it. How have you been, Maria?"

"I have *wilted* in your absence, my sweet. Too strongly do you remind me of the sun to my flower."

"Well, it is true that flowers are easier to look at than the sun," Anthony chuckled.

As she strode towards him, several other women emerged from behind their respective corners. Jim barely noticed them—the closer he was to Maria, the harder it was to concentrate. And yet, despite the openness they displayed towards one another, Maria was not someone Anthony saw in his future, in a different relationship than what they had now, at least. He liked to remain professional with her...while perhaps having a shifted definition of "professional" than other people.

"You are very easy to the eye, Señor Anthony," she cooed. "But in truth, I do want to know what you are doing in Colón. Not out of an issue of territory, of course, but because I am curious. You did not radio ahead, darling."

"I was in too much of a hurry. I had to overtake that ship."

"Ah yes, that wonderful speedboat of yours," and her eyes blazed as she remembered—or perhaps fantasized about—a sailing trip with Jim. "Perhaps you could make up for our time spent in absence of each other by allowing me to take a ride on it. I could use such an adventure as a pick-me-up, after the boredom of my last engagement."

"What would that be, if I may ask? Certainly not hunting down this fellow."

"No, he was a bonus. I was just wrapping up when I saw this man—I could not ascertain if he was you or not, though those wonderful muscles of yours were familiar to me—chasing another man, and I thought it would be interesting to shoot the fleeing one with a little dart full of... dream syrup."

"Maria, you're too impulsive for your own good. You could have helped a murderer catch up with his victim."

"But you do not murder, darling, I know that—and were there to be a murderer, I would have simply put out his eyes and snapped his wrists. Inspired, of course, by your philosophy."

Jim did not find that very funny, so there was an awkward pause between them. But Jim could save a conversation as well as the world. "I'm here to stop this man. He's a victim of some sort of hypnotizing narcotic..."

He went on to explain the case in full.

Maria Flores' eyebrow arched. "This sounds very interesting indeed, *mi amor*. I have heard of these missing ships. Is there a chance that my girls and I can be of assistance to the road—or seas—ahead? It has been ever so long since you've spoiled me, after all, as I have said. I heard that you were south of the border recently, and you forget again about poor Maria."

"I remembered you, but didn't have a chance to reach you. So what I'm saying is..." And he turned away, to begin walking back to where he'd docked the *Comanche*. "...I'd love it you could join me."

The hearty, inspired laughter of the girls, upon hearing his words, was oftentimes a greater payment to Jim Anthony than any of the riches of the world.

• • •

Maria Flores ran a tight ship with her organization of female mercenaries, and that metaphor became literal when she set foot on the *Comanche*. The trio of assistants she'd brought with her were introduced (or reintroduced) to Jim Anthony. Elizabeth, the uncanny redhead, Madeline, the wily brunette, and Helen, the powerful blonde. By grouping these three as often as she did, Maria Flores explained something about her sense of humor. But also there were secret reasons behind the "perfect trinity" of hair colors. In addition to possessing every skill held by men, they also guaranteed a certain weakness in the males they faced. This weakness was easily described by saying that some men liked blondes, while others preferred redheads, and so on. This was a talent that gave Flores' army an extra plethora of successes besides the many they accumulated through skill alone. Beauty was a weapon against a world of men who laughed at them on first sight.

"You are very easy on the eyes, Señor Anthony."

They were dedicated to the pursuit of justice, and their word for justice was a matter of debate. They took down bad regimes, bad businesses, and indeed, bad citizens as well. The evil folk who forced people to sell their bodies, or to become murderers. They loved adventure in a way that even Jim sometimes had trouble understanding. In short, they were magnificent.

The ship passed through the Panama Canal and into the Pacific. Maria was at the helm, aiding Jim in plotting the course for their coordinates of destination. It was an excuse to be close to him, but he did not mind.

"So this boat, then, Jim," she intoned. "It is named for your people, the Comanche, yes?"

"My Nation today has around 20,000 members," Jim said proudly. "And many of us served in the Great War, as soldiers and cryptologists. Many of the stories of our contributions were buried, but I'm not shy in saying that the Comanche were and are heroes."

"They spawned you as well. You do them proud."

He paused. "I do my best."

Her smile faded then. "You are tense, darling. And when you are tense you are moody. Do not be so dramatic, I implore you. This voyage will be thrilling. And thrills—they are as central to your heart as your ancestry."

Jim was struck by the wisdom she was offering. For a split second he actually flinched from a greater sense of light and color flooding into his eyes. He knew this feeling well—it was happiness.

"You're very right, my old friend."

"I always am, sweetheart."

The open seas were ahead of him. And nothing could stop him now!

The course was set, and there was nothing left but apprehension. But now this apprehension was sweet. There was great danger ahead. Something perhaps beyond imagination. Something that could claim their lives. Something infused with the tangible sense of menace and the unknown.

Thank goodness!

When there were lulls, they spoke to one another. Jim's sixth sense once again was a mighty guide for the perils of the ocean. Through this time they mentally kept track of their course, and could estimate how long it would be until they entered the missing-ship area. And in this span of waiting, Jim learned that Madeline was studying theology, Elizabeth had won seven gold medals in long-distance running in England, and Helen was planning to take a trip out to Germany to carry out a "disappearing act" involving certain political leaders, which she claimed was a personal project.

It became rather a merry time, and so it was a shame when at last, Jim and Maria said in unison, "We're coming up on it!" They looked at each other, and shared one last laugh—one glimmering, innocent moment before going off to the front.

It was indeed so very much like war. But all of them, no matter their personal lives, were warriors.

Helen was the first to cry out—"A fog bank!" And indeed, the speedboat was embraced quickly in a monstrous cloud of fog. Jim dashed to the controls and slowed the ship's advance. At once, his senses were ablaze—his sixth one, but also his ordinary sense of smell.

"There's something wrong with it..." he said aloud.

"Yes, I smell it too!" Maria called to him. "I think that dreadful poison you mentioned—it is this fog!"

The bad air! Jim Anthony remembered the entranced man's words; the words of the man finally back in a reinforced prison, this time in Panama. He had been changed by the bad air. Maria was right. The ships must have gotten lost in this cloud of drugged gas. It was the will-sapping gas—if he and the ladies didn't suit up, they, too, would become slaves of the villain behind this!

But Jim Anthony was prepared as always. Aboard the *Comanche* there were supplies to keep one safe in situations such as these. Gas masks were available, with an external oxygen supply as well. He had five air tanks that went with an equal number of masks.

"Get below decks, and breathe as little as possible!" When he ceased speaking he cupped the fading fresh air with his hands and sucked it in deep, before leading Madeline at the fore, with Maria, Elizabeth, and Helen behind, down to where the mask and tanks were. He demonstrated how to set them up but they didn't need it. They were all quite accomplished at holding their breath, and they had used these masks before.

They were all safe—for now. Jim didn't have to explain the grim situation they faced in the present. There was limited oxygen in the tanks, enough for about three hours. That was all the time they had to solve this case.

● ● ●

For several more minutes, there was no threat to the adventurers aboard the *Comanche* besides the limited visibility of the fog. But Jim's vision, as distorted as it was by the gas mask, was doing a good job of piercing it, for now. Thus, at a distance that most could not dream of seeing, he began to see a black shape form. It could not be anything else, especially on the sea, but a ship. Maria Flores, however, set her hand on her shoulder, indicating she saw it too.

The *Comanche* slowed as it neared the vessel, and Jim turned to face Helen and Elizabeth. "There are grappling hooks below decks," he said. "We'll need them for boarding."

"Right away, commander," they both said. Their voices had sing-song qualities to them.

Jim detected a hint of humor in those voices—not a bitter sarcasm, but a genuine lightheartedness—which he admired. In that sentence, and how they had spoken it, the two girls had shown their dedication to service, while also taking tremendous joy, as their leader did, in what they were doing. Jim felt an urge then to become the worrier of the group, in the case this happiness and eagerness also meant carelessness. But he wouldn't act on this urge unless they needed it, for he didn't *want* to assume his compatriots were being careless. For now, he would be the same as them—content with knowing that one's ability suited one for the task at hand. He was always protected by his greatest wingman, which was himself. The girls, too, were protected by themselves as well as each other.

CLUNK. Maria Flores' grapple was the first to hit the metal deck of the ship. It dragged up and the claws clung with great strength to the deck railing. In a single elegant sweep, the soles of her army boots were swiftly climbing the salt-crusted steel. Madeline had also fired before Jim had a chance to. These girls were like coiled springs. Jim had two beautiful women at his side when he arrived on the side of the ship, and soon all five of them were aboard.

Jim had heard Maria cry out once he climbed over the railing. It was a cry of alarm to her girls, and for a moment it looked necessary. The deck was swarming with human forms, who would have been exposed for God knew how long to that drugged gas. But Madeline piped up. "Captains, it would seem as though these people are in the state of suggestibility—they are intrinsically harmless."

In the time it took for her to say this, Jim was able to assess that they had no standing orders. Many of them were hunched over, their arms limp in front of them, while some sat in seeming dejection at random places around the deck. "Thank God that they don't look starved," Elizabeth said then. "How long have they been here?"

"At least a week," Jim replied, remembering that that was when he heard about the lost ships. "They must have some sort of order that lets them take care of themselves with whatever food is aboard. Our friend in Panama must have been from this lot."

"Even if they are taking care of themselves, they need to be recovered so they do not starve," Maria Flores said seriously. "Jim, my lovely—I trust you have a radio aboard your wonderful ship?"

"Of course. I'll contact the U.S. Navy authorities near Jarvis Island, and recommend the proper provisions for a recovery...and I'll leave out any mention of you ladies. I understand how business can be sometimes and maybe it's best that my government doesn't know that you're with me."

Behind her gas mask, Maria Flores cherry lips broke into a grin.

As Jim descended the side of the ship, Helen approached Maria. "Surely this cannot be the end of our romp? I know you and Mr. Anthony have said *ships*, plural..."

Maria kept on smiling. "You are correct, my sweet. I believe there are three of the vessels in total. Each other further ahead of the others—perhaps deeper in this queer fog. *Perros del infierno*! This bank must stretch for many miles, and perhaps it has a nexus as its center...where it has even weirder effects..." It was clear she was letting her imagination have its way. But she *wanted* this case to become more bizarre.

Even without superhuman senses such as those boasted by Jim Anthony—she had the feeling she was going to get her wish.

• • •

No time was wasted in setting out for the second ship.

Already, Maria was counting her lucky stars, for indeed the fog only seemed to grow thicker—even as seconds became minutes, and minutes became nearly an hour. How such a chemical could be so widely distributed was beyond her. There were no winds to blow it in the directions to which it had spread. Presumably then it had been brewed specifically to do this.

Again, her eyes, and those of Jim Anthony, were hard-pressed, and they could see even less than before. This, combined with their time limit, began to make their hearts run faster, their breath harsher. Jim could *feel* the preparedness of his comrades radiating from them. For thinking that they could ever be even close to ill-readied showed Jim that *he* was the one with a lack of focus.

Sixty minutes had passed, and only 120 remained in their oxygen tanks. But through the fog, another dark shape could be seen. "Land ho!" Maria shouted jokingly. Again, Jim readied his grappling hook. But as they neared it, they all became simultaneously aware that this would be an encounter of a different sort. A collective choir of ragged screaming could be heard from the deck.

They couldn't see what exactly was happening up there, but they were about to find out! Maria and Jim were neck-and-neck in their scramble up. What met their eyes was a scene of bizarre horror.

The ship's crew and guests alike were dancing wildly in the fog, while screaming with what appeared to be a grotesque fusion of pain, horror, and rage. All of them were covered in sweat as if they had been forced to dance this orgiastic display for days. Yet the same uncanny passion that caused them to dance also gave them, it seemed, superhuman energy—or at least so Jim deduced. His immediate concern was that this was not a dance, but a seizure. The manner in which the victims were afflicted certainly seemed akin to that in just how agonized and unnatural it looked!

Jim's danger sense returned properly at last. These people seemed more like monsters, but he couldn't let himself think that—they were the victims here, and their weird actions were performed against their will. And now they were going to rush him and his friends. He knew it as certainly as he felt the sea air around him, felt it give promises that soon he would become like these victims. And sure enough—with a brief hesitation—the large hordes of people began to sprint towards the heroes!

"Protect yourselves, my beautiful ones!" Maria cried, to man and woman alike. From leather holsters, she and her girls drew their dart guns, and began to stun the encroaching masses. But soon their arms were targets for the lunatics, who continued their horrible screams and awkward steps of their wicked dance as they attempted to seize them. Only melee would save them now!

Jim, not having a dart gun of his own, had removed his belt and begun to use it and its weighted end as a whip—taking great care not to bludgeon his allies. He didn't want to use the weight on his foes either, though, because they could be hurt permanently. But it made a great crack through the air, which seemed to frighten the screaming mob. Unlike the will-sapped drones of the previous ship, these people possessed cunning, if disturbed, intelligence. Even now, the ones grappling with Maria's compatriots were trying to speak to them...

"Can't stop us...can't stop us..." they moaned. "Cannot stop the master, and his bad air...cannot stop it..."

They were like a dreadful swarm intelligence—all bound to the same creed of violence! But Elizabeth managed to break the grip on her arms that one man, a sailor, had placed on her. It was a Herculean effort, for again, despite the sweat soaking the afflicted people, they had a tremendous strength that had a seemingly supernatural origin, even if it truly was just the gas. Trembling hands were starting to try to pull away the gas masks of Madeline and Helen. But the redhead, upon obtaining her freedom, was not going to abandon her sisters! The kick she made was almost overzealous—these people would have to wear some casts for awhile after they were rescued. Yet for Elizabeth, this injury was worth it to protect the lives and sanity of those close to her. The other two spoke their thanks before springing upon the sundry men and women who were seizing their chief!

"Roses of my heart, I am fine!" Maria Flores protested. "Please, save Jim Anthony!"

Jim hardly needed saving. The belt and its noise still put a deep terror in his enemies. "Take it away!" they shrieked. "Please, master, do not abuse us, please!"

And Jim hesitated then. He hadn't considered that the villain behind this had perhaps already exposed his victims to physical torture. By threatening to beat them—was he too much like the villain himself?

And yet now they were upon him! Whether their fear was legitimate or a desperate collective ruse, it did not matter. No matter how the tan arms flexed and the tight legs kicked, the detective was caught.

Even as Helen was slamming haymakers left and right into his captors, however, Jim was performing yet another of his signature throws on a man attempting to sink his teeth into his shoulder. Heavily he slammed against the deck, but he'd been handled so as to prevent serious injury. Against her wishes, Maria Flores had been freed by Elizabeth and Madeline.

"We must flee, Jim!" Maria called out. "There's no sense fighting these poor people! They'll kill us, and we have to hold back in fighting!"

She was right, and he knew it—this was a battle they could not win, even if it was one they wanted to. "Down the grapples!" he cried. The mob kept trying to restrain them, to once again expose them to the gas. Madness, like misery, it seemed, desired company—which perhaps explained why the person behind this was doing it all in the first place!

Yet the scramble down the hooks was no longer an option, as the shrieking passengers saw fit to drop the hooks in the ocean. But all of them could dive, and dive they did. The air was split with the cannonball thunder of five bodies breaching the ocean's surface. Jim noted that the oxygen tanks were dragging them down, and both Madeline and Elizabeth were struggling against the weight of the water above them. Jim took Elizabeth by the arm and helped her to rise, and was diving down to reach Madeline too. But Maria Flores swam in front of him. She paused briefly when they were both below the unending deep, and she slowly raised a single finger for Jim to see—and waved this finger back in forth. Despite the mask, Jim could almost read her lips, "Watch out for yourself. My girls are *my* children."

Children wasn't exactly the correct word, of course, given the nature of their intimacy. It was hard to put in words—though Jim had been calling them sisters in his head, they weren't entirely like that. Nor were they like friends or like lovers. Sometimes Jim caught himself thinking he didn't understand this love. But he shared it with many of his allies—Tom Gentry especially—and so he did understand. With that in mind, he let Maria handle the task of saving her girl.

They were all back aboard the *Comanche* in time, and had set sail again. Jim and Maria were at the helm once more.

Once the screams of the ship became only a memory, Maria decided to take this time to explain her theory of there being a gas nexus, where it was denser.

"It seems logical that there'd be such a thing," Jim replied. "You're right— we *should* be wondering about what the gas does in its concentrated form."

"Yes...or worrying, more likely..." But the Spanish beauty's voice was suddenly cut off by a harsh cough. "Is there a way of telling how much air is left in these tanks, darling?"

"There is. Turn around..." But within the confines of his mask, Jim's face drained of color as he examined Maria's tank. "This can't be right. Your tank must have been damaged in the fighting, or the water pressure did something to it. You only have thirty minutes left." He turned to his back to her as well. "Quick, check mine." And he gestured to the meter, which measured both in volume and time.

"Also thirty minutes, or just about," Maria confirmed. "Santa Maria. We have to check on the girls, too."

And sure enough—they too had prematurely lost some of their air. Helen had the most, at 52 minutes remaining.

"I can't believe that the tanks were this faulty," Jim murmured.

"Perhaps sabotage was involved?" Madeline suggested.

"I keep the *Comanche*—and thus all the equipment aboard it—well hidden. But evidently not well enough, if someone did tamper with it."

"Why would they sabotage the tanks, though, and not the *Comanche* itself?" Elizabeth countered.

"Because they would want us to be exposed to the gas. This place is a trap for us. Or for me. I shouldn't have brought you out here—now there's not a chance of even the *Comanche* being able to escape, so wide is the cloud. No matter what happens, we'll be exposed to the gas, unless it dissipates, which I doubt it will if it's been out here this long."

"Excuse me, Mr. Anthony," Helen said suddenly. "We *wanted* to be out here. I thought we made that obvious! Your sense of responsibility is adorable, but ultimately unnecessary, at least in this case. I'm just wondering—what do we do now? If we're going to lose, and go insane like those poor people, what do we do?"

Jim thought for several moments before continuing. "I think a pastor maybe forty years ago said something about how 'what really matters is who we are in the dark.'"

Helen thought about this for a few moments. "Well. The deeper we get into this fog—the farther away the sun seems."

Jim glanced at the sky, as if confirming her words. "Deeper we go, then, to the very end."

No one on the ship would have done otherwise.

• • •

It didn't take so long for them to come upon the last boat. Having recovered the grapples, they were all ready. That readiness, that focus on the situation, was a coping mechanism—what would come to them in only a few short minutes was too hideous to properly describe. Such words would take on several meanings as the deadly minutes ticked by.

And for once, there was a change in the quintet of adventurers. There was a sickness, like nausea or vertigo, spreading amongst them. It could have merely been an effect of the air in their tanks becoming thinner, but it could also have been fear. They didn't condemn each other, for it would have accomplished nothing—and this fear was not illogical. Jim trusted Maria, and through her trusted the girls. Faith would be their guide as they crossed these last waters.

Jim could radio out, of course. But no one could come in time. Only a miracle could help them. And now, for what would probably be the last time, he heard his grandfather Mephito's words in his mind, in an almost incidental memory—and he couldn't even remember the exact phrasing. Something about how the actions of "those above" often manifested as accidents. He was ashamed that he'd let the actual sentence be worn to a vague nub in his mind, and he couldn't understand why he was recalling this insight in the world of spirits at this particular moment.

But remembering his grandfather gave him a tiny sliver of hope. As ever, the answer seemed to be hidden in his ancestry. He could not let down the spirits of his parents, and he could not bring shame to his grandfather.

He knew he would not.

They were upon the final ship now. The grappling hooks fired for the last time, and swiftly, they all ascended to the ship's deck.

"I'm realizing, lion of my heart," Maria Flores said to Jim. "That there is no guarantee that the maker of this Satanic gas is aboard this ship. We've been losing our wits—why would he choose to stay in his own devil-cloud?"

"There was a chance to find a clue if he wasn't here. But I figured that perhaps he had an immunity to his product. Or maybe he thought he was immune."

"W-what would have become of him then? If he were not immune, that is?"

"I don't know. Maybe the gas stops its work at insanity. But as we discussed, there may be other effects. Maybe…"

And the detective's lips ceased to move. Maria became aware that his pupils were shrinking, in response to something he saw. She caught her first glimpse of what he was looking at in the glass of his lenses even before she heard the initial noise. She had to see for herself. Whirling around with a gasp, it was almost impossible to conceive what was happening before her eyes.

There were five men and one woman bursting through the metal of the deck. Their hands had broken fissures in the surface and now, beefy fingers were forcing these cracks open. The air was cluttered with the whine of the metal being shredded, and the ship, despite its great size, began frantically rocking once those within had gotten without. The persons involved were able to do this because they had been *transformed*—twisted by what Maria Flores had called the "devil-cloud." They were scarcely recognizable as human now. They were like the Giants of Genesis, and like those ancient beasts, these former humans were the very definition of monsters!

Their flesh was stretched thin from the force of their growth, which caused them to tower over thirty feet. Some of their skin had torn and was red from blood, and where it wasn't it was covered in boils. It was clear their mutation had been mental, as well. They were screaming in that horrible chorus from the ship before, which echoed loudly across the sea due to their enlarged throats. The occasional tinkling giggle of the lunatics was here a rich gurgling sound that was a perversion of laughter.

The most terrible part of these monsters to the heroes was that they represented that awful future that stood before them like a great cliff. Within hours, perhaps, they would become the kin of these foul things.

Each of the adventurers cried out their respective names for their deities. Even Jim. But the shouts were brief, and swiftly they recovered their senses—those senses which they had fought so hard to refine. And together, they were powerful.

Jim Anthony and Maria Flores lunged as one towards the monsters, leading the climactic charge. But they split and each other took on one of the giants—the Spanish beauty at a range, and the Irish-Indian sleuth with his belt at the ready up close. Above them were arches formed by the legs of these beasts, as three of them strode over to engage the girls, who similarly were drawing dart guns and knives. Their own cries tried to drown out the shrieks of the titans, but even if they could only be faintly heard the passion in them gave them strength.

Maria had taken one, and each of the girls had their own. But that meant that two—what had once been a bald man with a snaggletooth and a middle-aged woman—were left to attack Jim. In the darkness of his gasmask he smirked. This was how his story was meant to end. Against unspeakable odds, doing the right thing, with his friends. That was always to be his destiny!

But in the thrill of the fight, it almost felt like maybe there was still some reason to hope. He didn't know for sure. Adrenaline could make one cocky, he knew that for certain.

And yet, *God*, did it feel good to knock a punch into the creature's jaw!

Underneath the screams he could hear the cracks of Maria's group's dart pistols discharging rapidly. They had rather large cartridges, it seemed, but they were shooting to no avail. Either the skin of the changed ones was thick enough to deflect the shots, or the darts weren't reaching the right nerves or vessels to deliver the knockout drugs. But still, they were not afraid.

Helen was the first to lunge at one of the beasts with her glinting, military-grade dagger. The scream of her target was one purely of pain, and thus its notes were finally a break from the lunatic gibbering. The young woman's face flashed with satisfaction, then with pity—and finally with some degree of defeat. The other girls, and Maria, had followed her actions, but they, too, were coming upon that terrible question: how could they defeat these things with mere knives?

Jim wasn't having much luck either. His bolo-whip cracked through the air like fireworks, and it was leaving harsh red bruises on the exposed legs of his attacker. The clothes of the victims had not grown with him but for the most part the giants had their dignity.

As his duo of targets backed away from him, their weight was rocking the ship, and the detective had to fight hard to keep his balance. He still wasn't going to give up. He charged them again—perhaps he could cause them to fall overboard. They seemed rather heavy, though, and Anthony didn't know if the poor brutes could swim. If they wanted to save these victimized people, the fight was not one they could win. Jim cursed the man responsible...

The one responsible! That was right—Jim had considered he was aboard. Perhaps below, where their current foes had been waiting for signs of intruders before ripping through to the surface.

"Maria!" he cried. "Can you hold them off?"

"Where are you going, my darling?"

"I'm looking for the mastermind down below. Please, you and the girls have to hold them off!"

"I'm going with you, Jim!"

"Don't, Maria! The other three are going to need you while I..."

But with a spontaneous swiftness, the colossus Maria had been fighting swung down his great arm, and knocked her flat against the deck.

"*Maria!!*"

From where she had fallen, she stumbled to her feet, spitting out blood and perhaps a tooth. "Go, Jim Anthony!"

The words were simple, but were all he needed.

Descending the stairs he reached the lower decks, and ran as quickly as he could through the luxury halls of the liner, trying each of the doors that he came across. Most of them were locked, and within the rooms he could hear moans of some kind. He didn't want to fixate on what awaited him behind these sealed doors—not now, at least.

There were no clues in any part of the ship that Jim visited—until he went down one more deck. Here, the fog was a lot thinner, and yet the horror didn't let up. There were several people standing in the hallway, and they, too, were covered with the monstrous flesh of those above. Yet they were not much larger than average people. When Jim discovered them they had been standing rigid, with their arms pinched to their sides, their blank deformed faces staring at the ground.

But as soon as Jim went amidst them, their faces looked up at him, and split with wide grins. Then, as one, they gave a high pitched shriek and rushed him!

Jim raised his fists, even as his breath was becoming ragged.

What happened next was more akin to a dance than a fight—it was a more orderly dance than that of the lunatics from the second ship. But with the threat shadowing him, Jim's concentration was at its peak. His knowledge of the body was absolute, as it always had been from his years of study. His arms and legs weaved in and out of the spaces between the respective limbs of his foes. Silently, his hands or feet would gently twitch, only brushing against a certain bundle of nerves or cord of muscle. And the targets had no choice but to collapse, even with madness and mutation empowering them. They wouldn't feel any pain no matter what state of mind they were in.

And yet two of them must have taken more of the bad air than the others. They resisted the first strike Jim laid on them as he dove through the crowd. Jim whirled around in slight confusion, and lashed out against points in their legs, which would cause those limbs to buckle. But they shrugged this off as well, and their screams oscillated in a way that sounded to Jim like taunting laughter—just like that of the maddened giants above. If they were more durable, so be it.

Dancing again, he threw a snap-kick at the mottled creature's head which knocked him back—but he didn't even bruise. A jab with his elbow sent the other away as well. He had replaced his belt and had to get it off again—thankfully his reflexes were still sharp. Twirling it over his head, he didn't waste any time in taking any chance he had, like a predator. And yet such a metaphor saddened him. He had let his repulsion by these unfortunate souls overwhelm him, and he had let himself forget, as he had begun to do before on the previous ship, that these people were victims. He realized now that indeed, he must have breathed of the gas, due to his mask being yanked for a moment or damage to his air-tank.

And *that* was the secret to the madness behind the drug! It created paranoia and apathy at the same time. This in turn spawned a frenzied desire to defend oneself against these others—these invaders, these *others* who were no longer worthy of empathy. It was fear of the unknown turned to hatred! And it was now overtaking Jim Anthony.

His air was almost out, and he knew that it was the same for the women on deck, if it was not too late for them already. With one of his final breaths, the detective at last knocked down the remaining two opponents. He didn't have time to check if they were dead or not, but he could see that they were still breathing. He envied them! They had nothing to worry about, while his suffering was just beginning. They were already mad, while he had to look forward to his memories of his loved ones being supplanted only with that hatred.

But he did still have that little bit of air. He ran further down the hallway, holding his breath as long as he could. For a moment it looked like his luck was up at last. At the hallway's end, however—there was a lone door that had been broken open!

Jim dashed inside, and found a room reduced to ruins by one of the raging madmen. Inside there was an elegant desk beside a silk-sheeted bed. The desk had been shattered in two by a sturdy blow, and there were many scientific papers scattered on the floor. It didn't take long for Jim to notice that these notes were chemical formulae!

As he got inside he examined the desk. One of the first things that caught his eye was the shattered frame of a worn photograph. Besides it was a black leather case containing a passport.

It was a fortuitous discovery, and though Jim's eyes were blurring, he could see the name on it from afar: "James Q. Meteon, PhD."

Professor James Q. Meteon! Jim hadn't even considered his name before at all in this case, and it was remarkable that he hadn't done so. The Professor had gained renown and infamy alike for use of advanced machinery to control the winds. He had experimented with wind-generated power—an admirable goal, Jim thought—but his machines often had a particular amateurish quality to them. One of his devices only released toxic fumes instead of controlling the air. He was arrested when an elderly woman whom he was demonstrating the machine to had choked to death under these fumes—everyone else at the demonstration was merely knocked unconscious.

Meteon slowly lost his sanity, and according to some acquired a drug habit. Hashish, or perhaps opium. It filled his mind full of awful delusions, and he was last known to have been experimenting with various gas-weapons that had been used in the Great War.

The man in the photograph was Meteon, and the man up above—one

His arms and legs weaved in and out...

of the thirty-footers—was also that man. He was the bald one with the protruding tooth. Meteon *had* been consumed by his own formula, which created a weird hormonal imbalance that was somehow the source of both the physical and mental aberrations. The foolishness behind that exposure tipped Jim off that he had missed the Great Spider again—once more, he recognized that someone smart enough to control both the Flame Wizard and Baron Sturm wouldn't have done this to themselves.

No, the chess-master was *still* out there! It was too horrible for him to rationalize. But he distracted himself with an even more pressing fact: he was now absolutely out of air.

There was no point in wearing the gas mask anymore, but before removing his mask he bent low to the ground. Like smoke in a fire, there was purer air the lower one got. He had noticed it when he was wandering in it, and so when he was starting to choke because he was wearing the mask he ducked low to the ground and sucked in a deep breath.

From this position another sheet of paper caught his eye. He didn't exactly know why it seemed important, but as his vision settled on the various chemical symbols on the sheet, he had some inkling of what it could be. A quick assessment of the elements used made him realize that this was a formula for a drug affecting the endocrine system. Could it be the gas...? There was a chance. Even if it was just the earliest batch of notes for the gas, Jim could work with it. He memorized the location of this single sheet of paper as he finished filling this lungs with air.

Using this last gasp, he sprinted up the stairs and was soon back on the deck. The girls looked to be in bad shape, but they were retreating even as they removed their masks.

"Jim, I'm so sorry," Maria Flores said. "We couldn't defeat them, and we..." She cut herself short, realizing that she and her army weren't alone in having had to remove their masks. "So this is the end, then, yes?"

"I don't know," Jim replied. "I found out that the likely culprit is a man named Professor Meteon." And he went on to explain his discoveries. In the background, the giants continued to bellow, but as they were all ducked in the entrance to the deck stairs, the enraged titans lost sight of them.

"That's wonderful news, though, wolf of my passion!" Maria cried. "You can devise any antidote to the gas! We just need to find a way out of here."

"There is no way out of here anymore. We know that for sure."

"But it's not, Mr. Anthony," Madeline cut in suddenly. Jim couldn't help the confusion on his face.

"She's right. We can still defeat the giants," Elizabeth agreed. "I still have a couple of knockout darts left. We realized that if we cut their legs it will give an opening for the darts to kick in."

The detective had to think for a few moments. "If we don't attempt to stop them, the Navy may simply see fit to torpedo the ship, which will kill the people aboard. They may do that even if we can somehow intervene... but we still have to try to minimize the damage.

"I have no idea when the gas will start affecting us. It could be minutes— even seconds. But we have to *try*..."

His voice caught in his throat. Maria and her girls just nodded at him, and they went to work.

In places where growing had stretched the skin till it tore open, and where they had already cut, the women fired the remainder of their darts. The giants went on the offensive again, but once more they were slug- gish. Perhaps the people they once were held them back. But Elizabeth, Helen, and Madeline did not have many of their darts, and even as they injected them into the open wounds, at first it seemed as though nothing would work. Nonetheless, Jim was studying the body language of the gi- ants. Though corrupted by their insanity, it was still legibly human, and that meant Jim's mastery of reading such language still applied. They *were* slowing down, and becoming dizzy, it seemed. Perhaps they *would* col- lapse. Perhaps...

And just then, one of them did fall. Rocking the ship of course. But Jim yelled over: "We've got to secure them so they don't fall overboard!" The one who had fallen had done so along the length of the ship, fortunately, but the other might not be so lucky. As the wooziness overtook the altered people, the adventurers scrambled to urge them to fall in such a way that they would not plunge into the dark depths.

Because there were five giants and five of them, they each took one— Jim stood at the feet of Professor James Meteon. His eyes reflected none of the intelligence he had once possessed, and would maybe possess again. Jim's disgust had been replaced entirely with pity. How judgmental even Jim Anthony could be! He was not so repentant of his judgment as to forgive Meteon for unleashing his terrible chemical, for whatever rea- son he may have had—the suffering the people he had victimized would haunt them forever. Jim rationally knew that it was a fact that many of the changed folk here would spend much of their lives in mental institutions, and this rationality cloyed out hope.

Hope! Now *that* was a concept in these desperate times. Obviously enough it was on the minds of all of the heroes assembled here, and just as clearly on their lips as well.

"What do we do before the end?" Maria Flores articulated at last, when all the giants were unconscious and secured. They had asked it so many times before, and yet each time, the fight in them made them ask it again.

Jim said nothing at first. Just as he opened his mouth, however, a curious feeling came over him—the stimulation of his sixth sense was fading away. The fog was as thick as ever, but his mind was telling him that the danger was finally ending.

He wondered if this was somehow a premonition of his death, as if something was trying to tell him that the danger would be fading indeed—all danger, forever. Yet all the same, it was one final rejuvenation for him. "You're familiar with karma, right, all of you?" he asked.

"In a way, *si*. It's something like what you Americans say—what goes around, comes around?" Maria replied.

"That's a simplified way of saying it, but...yes. Now—would you say that we've done good today?"

The answers came slowly at first. "We tried our best," Madeline said. "So yes."

"We did not harm innocent people unnecessarily," Helen said. "I'd say so."

"Let's not forget the man we captured in Panama," Elizabeth chimed in. "We didn't stop the whole network, but we stopped *him* from hurting more people."

"We haven't been perfect, but only evil is perfect," Maria Flores said. And she grinned. "*Si*. We have done well today."

"It's not just in the Eastern philosophies—Buddhism, Hinduism, Taoism, Jainism, Sikhism—that one can find karma, y'know," Jim then continued. "I think it's a key principle of the American dream that good deeds make good rewards, too."

They didn't speak.

But a moment later, the air was split with a sound besides that of the sea air.

It was faint at first, and yet familiar. The louder it got, the clearer it was. And indeed, they all knew the sound—for after all; they had all heard an auto-gyro before.

"We have to get its attention!" Maria cried out, but Jim just grinned.

"That won't be necessary, my dear. I know that bird!"

Under the blades of the gyro, the gas was scattering—it was reforming, but pockets of fresh air formed for a few moments. When air came over the deck of the cruise ship, a lightness returned to the lungs of the adventurers. And Jim's smile only got wider, because even though his eyes were weakened by seeing the sun again, he could see who was within the cockpit of this particular auto-gyro.

"Hi, Jim!" Tom Gentry called out.

Jim Anthony's emotions were beyond words, and he didn't immediately return his old friend's greeting. But the surprise wasn't over, for suddenly there was another figure visible within—a shorter man, with a European face.

"Dawkins!" Jim cried. And at once, his eyes moistened. There was no chance of him being able to control the overwhelming emotion he felt when he saw that the smallish butler was healthy—fit enough to travel.

"You mentioned it before you took off, remember? The auto-gyro, that is," Tom was saying. "We both healed up quick, and got down here at once."

"I have many questions for you, my dear friend. But I'll wait till we're all aboard." The detective looked over his shoulder. "Ladies first."

Soon the girls of Maria Flores were aboard, and Jim had his foot in when he remembered something. "One second!" And held his breath as he went back to the room of Professor Meteon. He recovered as many of his notes as he could, and returned. "Let's get out here. Sorry for the holdup." And he perused the notes for a moment. "Not only can I reverse the hormonal effects of the gas from these notes, but I can create a spray which will counteract the fog."

"That's wonderful, my darling! I didn't doubt you for a second," Maria said. Deep weariness was in her face, but her joy was genuine.

"But how did you manage to swing this rescue?" Helen asked Tom. "We didn't have any sense of where we were."

"The radio on the *Comanche* was on! And I can trace that signal from the controls," Tom said.

Jim was confused. "I didn't turn the radio on, Tom."

"Maybe not on purpose. But when we'll recover the *Comanche*, I'm sure it will still be on. It's actually on now."

Jim simply nodded. But suddenly, that phrase of his grandfather's came back in full. "The spirits do not help one directly. But they *do* help us in our darkest hours, and that is why there are accidents," Mephito had once told him. To Jim's Christian friends, they had their own iteration—about God working in mysterious ways.

Jim had no idea what his own beliefs were, but he was thankful to be alive. And things always did seem to come around, when they went around.

But all the same, as he had in his prior cases, he took on a dour expression. And this was not noticed by the Spanish woman who had conquered so many monsters on this day. "What ails you, sweet one?"

"It's still not over," he replied. "All this fighting, all these deaths—and it's still not over."

"But you saw it yourself, darling!" Maria Flores said. "The man behind this was driven mad, turned into a freak, by what he unleashed! It *is* over!"

"Yet the man behind this would be too brilliant to not properly test his substance. No, Meteon, or the man we assumed was Meteon, was another pawn. Like Sturm, like Kallinikos. This is just the beginning, Maria." He sighed wearily. "And if I'm allowed to be a little theatrical...I think this will only come to a head when the whole earth itself is at stake!"

End of Part Three

MADNESS IN THE CAVES

Calamity and devastation were the new laws of the land.
The laws were scarcely new—these nations had been struck before and would be struck again by the agony of famine and disease and Empire, by warfare from both within and without. Not just here in Cameroon, but all over Africa. Cameroon had seen some of the worst, and here, again, death was walking. It was only new in that this particular brand of it had not been seen prior.

The sky was rent with apocalyptic clouds. Below, red lights danced in a way that seemed to almost mock the crying, screaming crowds below. They were the lights of flames both close and distant—hungry, all-devouring flames, which turned the remains of the village to smoke and ash. This ash scattered through the air like snowflakes, which fell alongside by debris smacking hard into the charred soil. These ashes still burnt hot enough to singe the feet of the crowds, though the pain in their hearts and the shock in their minds drowned out the damage these remnants caused to their soles.

Only a fraction of the victims were looking into the hideous crater that was once their home. But those select few were stunned further, this time into utter silence. Some of the ashes on the ground were stirring, as if they were not clumps of ruined wood, but tiny insects, like the flies that swarmed in the afternoon heat. The ones in the air slowly began to join them, until great quantities of ashes filled the bottom of the pit the eruption had opened. Among the witnessing crowd was Dr. Muteba Muamba, who was aiding the wounded. His eyes locked fast on the stirring coals, trying to find any clue to what could be causing their weird behavior. Yet even with his great experience—it did seem to be the work of ghosts!

The ensuing seconds, however, would reveal that these ghosts, if spirits they were, had curious motives. Many hauntings arose from the departed supposedly seeking the attention of one still living. And if these ashes were the voice of someone or something long dead, there was indeed great portent behind their identity. For slowly, they were forming letters...and the letters were forming words.

Dr. Muamba allowed himself a rare gasp. And at once, he excused himself from the rest of his colleagues, who remained unaware of the message within the crater. There was a radio nearby in the jeep that had brought him here from Yaoundé. As distasteful as it was to him, he knew he needed to contact the British authorities. They could contact the United States, and it was only a matter of a short time before the man they needed would be here to see—*that*—with his own eyes.

"This is Dr. Muteba Muamba calling the British Army," he said. "Repeat, this is Dr. Muamba. I need to speak with Lieutenant Stevens immediately."

There was a very long wait, but Muamba didn't give up. He repeated his message several times until he was interrupted by a disdainful voice: "This is Lieutenant Stevens of the British Cameroons. What's going on, Muamba?"

"I'm at the village of Buru, where that bomb supposedly went off. There's something strange here, and I can't explain it."

"I'm sure we'll have time to investigate it shortly, Dr. Muamba. Now please, just calm down and tend to the wounded like your job says you should."

"No, Lieutenant. The ashes here...are alive. Or seem alive."

There was silence for awhile. "Listen, doctor. There are many things which even you do not understand. I'm sure it's absolutely nothing."

"*You* are the one who should listen, Stevens. The ashes have been animated by some sort of chemical process that's beyond anything I've ever seen before in a laboratory. Somehow, they have been conditioned to...to form words. Or rather, a name. I need you to contact the United States, and give a warning to the man whose name they spelled."

Again, silence reigned for a time, until again, the disbelieving voice of Stevens returned. "What is this name, then, Muamba?"

And Dr. Muamba grinned, because he knew he'd have a miniscule vengeance in the shock this name would bring to Lieutenant Stevens. "The name is Jim Anthony. Someone is trying to get the attention of the American explorer, Jim Anthony."

• • •

There are some minutiae that don't deserve attention, even for one as meticulous as Jim Anthony. There are too many details in the world for most people to absorb, and life is too short to take them all in. Yet for someone to attack guiltless people, to kill so many, was definitely no minor incident, and while Anthony was loath to pay attention to such a fanatical killer, he had no choice if he wanted to protect other innocents.

When Jim received notice of the terrible act committed in Cameroon, and his association with it, he wasted no time. Both he and his Irish pilot, the ever-faithful Tom Gentry, were present in the Penthouse, Jim's apartment headquarters in New York, when the summary of the case was passed to him from Dr. Muamba, through Lieutenant Stevens. "...and so it does rather sound like you should get down here right away."

"You have nothing to fear about that, Lieutenant. I'll be in Cameroon in a few..."

That last word was cut off to Tom, as he was already getting the car ready to head out to the *Thunderbird*—the magnificent super-plane of the Super-Detective. Jim really didn't take any time. He'd had the *Thunderbird* prepped with his equipment for several months now, following the business of the Pacific gas cloud of Professor Meteon. Meteon had been overcome with his own drug-gas, which had caused him to mutate into a titanic and insane monster. He, along with those he transformed into beings like himself (or else slaves carrying out preprogrammed tasks of crime around the world), had been cured by Jim's own mastery of chemistry, and was now sane, though he wasn't willing or able to talk about his employer.

And yet Meteon, along with Alexander Kallinikos and Baron Sturm, were possibly mere minions of yet another scientist who controlled an enormous crime network. Rather like Jonathan Wild and his gang, or the servants of Adam Worth, the Napoleon of Crime. Jim had been waiting for around three months in total for another movement. He thwarted some small rackets and scams in the holdover, but now he knew the villain had struck again.

He was probably revealing himself, too. To control ashes as the Lieutenant had described demonstrated an almost godlike power over matter. This was the master villain, alright. Jim knew it in his bones, and he knew it by way the sixth sense that pulsed in his brain, that detected danger.

Yet this particular stimulation of the danger-sense was coming from something more direct than this cry for attention. Once Jim and Tom reached the Waldorf-Anthony's garage, Tom discovered hurriedly that...

"The engine's not turning over."

Jim's face lit with concern. "Let's look under the hood. Quickly!"

And yet, as soon as the hood was opened, they saw the problem all too well. It looked as if someone had taken an acetylene torch to the machinery within—a gnarled and fused black mass was all that met their eyes. The car was junk now, and there was no time to speculate on who had done this.

Jim dove back into the car and turned on the radio. "This is Jim Anthony calling Donlevy at the *New York Star*. Repeat—Jim Anthony calling James Donlevy. Are you there?"

There were a few seconds of delay. But sure enough, the voice of *Star*'s editor came crackling back. "Jim?"

"Hello, Donlevy. Something's come up and I need one of your...publisher's favors."

"I-I'll do what I can on such short notice. But don't forget—we're a newspaper, not a weapons division."

Jim grinned, but it was brief. "I have my own armory, Donlevy, don't worry. I just want to borrow a car. Someone has been rather vicious to mine."

"I told you to cut back on those high speed chases, Mr. Publisher. I'll get someone to the Waldorf-Anthony in ten minutes."

Jim hesitated. "That's fine, Donlevy. Thank you." He knew that it would be proper to thank him further, but his desire to get on with his mission as soon as possible sometimes overshadowed his desire to be polite. And the sheer thrill of that action—or even the hint of it—would sometimes tempt him to abandon human conventions entirely to pursue that thrill and nothing else. After all, he'd consistently proven his worth to the world where he could step into the role set up by a certain German philosopher some fifty years prior. But all the same, he couldn't help but feel as if such a thing was evil. Some (but not all) conventions were the building blocks of morality, and therefore by stepping away from them he would risk the collapse of his ethics. Everything thus had a consequence—even something as small as thanking one's ally properly.

Tom Gentry recognized that Jim was thinking over these concepts and others as they waited for the car, and thus remained silent. But the garage became suddenly chilly in Jim's presence. It was easy for the pilot to deduce Jim's own conclusions about what these rumblings meant, as far as who they were fighting, and he offered a silent prayer of sorts that this case would end with the defeat of the puppeteer. He was beginning to become sincerely worried that his old friend was perhaps becoming, well, corrupted.

If Jim Anthony slipped into darkness he could be stopped. But not without a fight. And Lord—that fight wouldn't be any different than any other that he'd put up over the years.

Tom hadn't read Nietzsche, however, and thus held onto the belief that the super-man was bound to the man inside, or else, to men beyond himself. Even if one destroyed their inner humanity, one could still be saved by one's human friends. Again and again he was reminded that he was not just Jim's friend, chauffeur, pilot, and bodyguard, he was also his anchor, holding the mighty destroyer of the brain that lurked behind that tanned skin docked at the harbor.

The car came in four minutes, rather than ten, and the two didn't waste any time climbing into it—save for a quick jab of Jim's arm towards the driver. Tom caught him doing this and the rushed thanks that came about, and his curiosity was piqued as the car bolted out onto the road. "What did you say to him?"

"I think Donlevy may have had to send one of his reporters, and this is his car. So...I slipped him a Franklin."

"*Gee-man-ee*, Jim! Don't you know there's a Depression going on?"

"Then I shouldn't tell you I gave him five Franklins."

"Don't do that too often, my friend. People may start thinking you're generous."

Jim laughed then—and it was sincere laugh. He relished it, knowing that there wouldn't be many ahead.

It didn't take long to reach the airport where the *Thunderbird* had landed, and they wasted no more time sprinting aboard, with a power of propulsion that would have perhaps broken world records had there been the right circumstances. They were at the edge of the adventure—its liminal line was coming like the dawn.

And yet it smelled curiously like smoke.

"Oh, no," Tom said swiftly. And his face was twisted with blind rage. "No, no, *no!*"

The giant's cry of anger broadcast to Jim what had happened before he saw it for himself. There had been smoke in the cabin, as a result of the same acetylene that had afflicted the car. He gave an almost casual sigh before horrible implications began to set in. Perhaps some of Jim's own trusted employees had betrayed him, using their unique access to his fleet to spread sabotage. Even if the perpetrators had forced their way in, it showed they were able to do so without alerting him or any of his employees. And it showed that they were toying with him, as many of his foes had done now. He needed to get to Africa quickly, and that was no longer possible—his speedboat, the *Comanche*, was named in part for the great speed of the people of the Indian tribe to which he belonged, but it would still take great time to cross the Atlantic.

Where did he go from here?

Jim's eyes flashed about the ruined cockpit, even as misery—only half-real—touched the voice of Tom Gentry. "Look what they've done to my baby...I'll never fly her again!"

"Don't worry, Tom. No matter what's damaged, we can rebuild her. I could even construct another just like her and not have to worry about my pocketbook too much..." And as he finished that sentence, his eyes locked finally on the flight controls, and those same orbs lit up with understanding.

"Almost too easy," he said then. "But I suppose it's all part of the game...?"

"What's up, Jim?" Tom asked.

"They shot the controls, too."

"Shot them? Why? That torch took good enough care of it as it was..."

"What's the first code you can think of?"

"Code? Like...like Morse code?"

"Yes, absolutely. That's the one. The bullet holes," and he pointed at them emphatically, "are dots and dashes. And I've already translated them."

Tom wasn't surprised. "What—do they say then?"

Jim's face almost looked simply irritated. But he was probably making himself look just irritated to disguise the fact that was plain enough for both of them once he spoke the translation. "'Passenger plane.'"

They didn't say anything at first. Eventually, however, Jim's priorities won out over his tongue. "Tom, I—want you to stay here and repair the *Thunderbird*, and follow me to Africa with reinforcements if I don't report back. You saved me when Maria Flores and I were chasing those ships, and I may need that last hope again. Please, don't decline this assignment. I need to go alone, but I know I'm not truly by myself in this."

Those last few words convinced Tom of his friend's safety. Tom raised his hand, and Jim shook it. But Tom pulled him in close, and held him like men in the trenches of the Great War held each other before they went over the top.

"Good luck."

Jim asked the airport employees to inform the *Star* about the location of the borrowed automobile. From there he was able to find that there was a flight to Cameroon later that afternoon.

But he knew there was a reason why he had been forced to take this flight. If he was going to get to Africa with due speed, he would need to leave today—and this was the only Cameroonian flight. There was something that was going to take place on that plane that would put people in danger. Jim insisted upon making this point to the airport staff.

"I'm sorry, sir—even with your authority, I cannot order this flight to be made private for you," the clerk was saying. "The U.S. ambassador to the Congo is aboard. He has urgent business and is being transported from Cameroon to the Congo."

"I take it there are no other flights to Africa the ambassador could take? I would only ask this as a matter of equal urgency."

"I'm afraid not, sir." And the clerk was beginning to become irritated with Jim.

The key issue was that he had no definitive proof that there was danger. The clerk's manager was nearby, as was the owner of the airport, but neither of them looked particularly impressed. And Jim didn't have time to get higher authorities involved, much less persuaded.

Silently, he came to the realization that he would have to defend the passengers of this plane if something did happen. There would be no rest till he reached Cameroon.

• • •

He sipped gently at a martini. Jim Anthony could hold his liquor, and sometimes he did let himself feel the positive effects. In this case he needed relaxation—the rigidity in his body created by his anxiety would inhibit him more in combat than the minor motor impairment of a single drink.

It had been a few hours, and nothing had happened. There wasn't even any turbulence, and as the alcohol warmed him he wondered if perhaps he had been paranoid. And yet he still felt the low hum of his sixth sense—it purred in his mind like a kitten, but one with wicked claws. He decided it would be a good time to meditate.

And yet, as soon as his eyes drooped closed—the purr became an anguished screech!

His eyes snapped open, and he saw the passengers in the row before him undo their safety belts and stand up. He, and everyone else, in fact, hadn't noticed that their faces, those of old men, were loose and rubbery like masks. Because they *were* masks—faces of old codgers that suddenly seemed deeply ugly to Jim. It didn't help that somehow, they already had rifles in their hands.

Jim didn't say a word, but an old woman from behind saw the same sight. And she started screaming, awakening a riot as she did so. Others, male and female alike, screamed in horror at the sight of the masked men standing menacingly. Jim's hands went fast to the harness of his safety belt—and also to the button on the buckle of the belt wrapped around his waist. The hijackers didn't seem to notice loosening of either. As he rose to his feet he slipped his belt through the loops of his jophur pants, and at once it was no longer a belt—it was a bolo!

Soon the crowds cried out again, but in joyous surprise—they recognized the sturdy form of Jim Anthony, and knew to keep their heads down.

The belt lashed out once with a crack, and two men were down at once. Jim kept the bolo twirling above his head as he locked eyes with his enemy, underneath his mask. "You know who I am. Surrender immediately."

At least one of the masked men dropped his rifle, and went down on his knees.

Yet from the other compartments of the plane, out sprang eight other men similarly disguised—some disguised convincingly as young people, too. "I'm sorry for this, everyone!" Jim cried out. "But keep your heads low as you've been doing and you'll escape this unharmed!"

And when he cracked his whip again, he called out to the intruders. "Again: I offer a chance to surrender. In the name of the United States of America! Surrender!"

They did back up for a second—but then one of their number decided to chance it. And that was the catalyst for everything else. There was no chance for peace. Eight men had to be dropped for the passengers to be safe.

And among those eight, one wouldn't find the name of Jim Anthony.

As he had before, Jim utilized gracefulness to accomplish his goals. A pirouette in one direction resulted in his targets falling like ninepins—he had managed to strike their pressure points. All but one had fallen, and he was used to some being able to resist his cunning jabs. But he used another of his mastered skills on them by seizing the bodies of the standing men— two from the front—and hurling them at the others—who numbered four, and who came from the tail-end of the plane.

They had better reflexes than a lot of the dopes he'd gone up against lately! When they saw a man's heavy unconscious body rocketing towards them, they ducked, all save one of them, who was slammed hard against the floor. "Watch for turbulence!" Jim cried then.

The three who were left kept coming, and Anthony decided to greet them with his fists. A left, a right, and another left. That was all it took.

And yet out of the three—two stumbled back up. That *impressed* Jim... but just barely.

They both dove forward to again be greeted by his fists. But another managed to jab into his collarbone. Jim had broken his collarbone long ago, and it was a medical fact that once that particular bone knitted, it became unbreakable. He was able to suffer this blow easily, and deal out another of his own.

That was enough. The last man was done just a second after the second-to-last.

Jim let out a single dramatic breath.

"Let me just get my carry-on and I'll cuff these guys," he said then. And he grinned.

The passengers smiled back, and then laughed—and then applauded. Jim felt a swell of pride over being able to rescue these people, for the people they were. He hadn't done it for personal gain—he had done it because it was the duty of all capable humans to protect the lives of those around them. By fulfilling that duty, it meant Jim Anthony the man won out.

That was good for him, and that goodness was fuel to his flames.

● ● ●

The flight passengers cried out "Thank you!" as Jim left their company, when they landed. Jim had been genuinely expecting fighter planes to attack the flight or something. He was happy they'd made it here as they had, and sorry to see the passengers go. He did want to try to keep in touch with some of them.

Here he was: in Cameroon, separated from Tom Gentry. That had been his choice; it was true, as he really did need the promise of that emergency backup. He didn't want to admit that maybe his enemy *wanted* him alone—with the aid of Tom Gentry, James Donlevy, Maria Flores, and many others, Jim had prevailed. As a solitary agent, however, his circumstances were possibly different.

He saluted the Union Jack as it waved on the back of the British vehicle driving towards him. "You must be Lieutenant Stevens!" Jim called out.

Stevens merely nodded, and did not react well to the detective's smile. "Get in the car," he said gruffly.

Jim nodded back, but only with some hesitation boarded the vehicle.

"How is Cameroon, Lieutenant?" Jim asked then.

"It's a bitter and cursed land. I long for England and its simplicity, and civilization. Here there are only savages."

"Yet I, Lieutenant, have heard a great many good things about the Cameroonians. Including our apparent mutual friend, Dr. Muamba."

...Anthony...greeted them with his fists.

"Dr. Muamba is a cur."

Jim suddenly took offense, and realized at once who Lieutenant Stevens was—a proud and staunch supporter of "the colonies." Empire was a popular concept even in, sadly, the United States, even if it went against the principle of "liberty and justice for all." He was condescending and biased against the people whom he merely viewed as British subjects. And Jim was reminded of the simple fact that Englishmen such as he, in the name of their Empire, had oppressed both his Irish and Indian ancestors. Was it any wonder that Jim Anthony was on the side of the Africans when it came to talk of colonies?

But he would let this pawn of Empire take him to the village. Dr. Muamba would be much more reasonable to deal with—a pleasure, in fact. Even American publications lauded his surgical skill and ability in fighting disease. He had identified two undiscovered bacilli and perfected a preservation method for organs during transplants, which worked most efficiently during heart transplants but could also be used for "lesser" surgeries. And he was still very young—younger than Jim, in fact, which meant he had a prosperous career ahead of him.

The drive was short, but it seemed longer with the tension between the two men. Nonetheless, Jim was often able to distract himself when he was forced into close company with people he didn't respect, and this time was no exception. He was mulling over Dr. Muamba's report again, and had to admit to himself that he was a tiny bit giddy. It would be invigorating to see what sort of chemical secrets this villain had just revealed. There was the Janus face again—the love of crime-fighting versus the seriousness of crime! He hated crime for the harm it did to innocents, but it seemed logical to him that that hate should carry over into his combat against injustice, simply due to the grievousness of that harm.

But before he could ponder this further, the Lieutenant spoke. "We're 'ere."

Jim looked out the window, and saw that the passing of these past few hours had not quelled the scale of the devastation at Buru. There was still horror and trauma in the faces of the survivors—the grief was nearly tangible. And nothing could kill the oppression of the sight of a ruined home. Jim Anthony was stirred deep within by this sight, and he walked lightly as he approached the remains of the village.

At the crater there was an African man standing clad in a lab coat and loudly giving orders to people in other such coats and scrubs, as well as white British soldiers, whose brows were knit with a not-so-quiet frustration. Jim didn't even have to ask—when the two men caught sight of each other; their hands were extending towards each other. In that intense handshake was a sense of brotherhood.

"Dr. Muamba," Jim said with a grin.

"Mr. Anthony! It's good to meet you at last," Muamba replied. "Let's waste no time."

"A sentiment I can get behind. Into the crater, then?"

"Yes, Mr. Anthony, but please, show tremendous respect. This pit is a cemetery."

Jim solemnly nodded.

Of course, he could see the message from the lip of the crater. The only reason why they were descending was, naturally, to examine the ashes directly. On his back, over the gray sweatshirt he had donned on the ride over, was a pack full of chemistry equipment—among other effects, things for which he had needed the NYPD commissioner's approval. But he wasn't ready to use those yet.

Muamba and Jim knelt near the ashes, and were at once puzzled by how smooth the edges of the giant letters seemed. Not only were the ashes controlled in an impressive way, they had been controlled with the precision of a master sculptor or surgeon. And yet they had been not fused into their shapes, and Jim was able to easily take some of the ashes and put them in a vial.

"Just a second," Jim Anthony said then. "And we'll know what this stuff is."

"You're going to test the chemistry of the ash right here?" Muamba asked.

"Yes. I have a hand-held spectrometer—well, a variant of one. I can identify the chemicals in the ashes from the spectrograph lines."

"That—that's incredible!"

Jim smiled. He didn't say it aloud, but he remembered the times when he had spoken similar words, when witnessing (by books) the genius of Tesla, Pasteur, Galileo...it was why he became a scientist in the first place. Perhaps in other circumstances he would have been a poet, and yet it had been those words—"That's incredible!"—that made him into who he was today.

Dr. Muamba, he had heard, had become a scientist both in a desire to help victims of poverty and to scorn European and American foundations who discouraged and fought against his career. The former desire, however, had always overshadowed the latter. Compassion over vengeance.

Muamba was looking closely on the display of the pocket spectrometer that had emerged from Jim's pack. "If I'm reading those elemental lines correctly," Jim began. "These ashes are the result of—the burnt material being chemically converted to plastic."

"How do you figure that?" Muamba asked, with a sliver of skepticism to his voice.

"Well. The building material...was not plastic. And this is a plastic. The sort used to build toys, almost—but with better memory..."

Muamba's eyes lit up. "That's how it retained its shape!"

"But how would it take on that shape to begin with? It's not like the plastic memory could be passed on chemically. You couldn't transfer that shape into another material, because the plastic is new."

"But what if you could, Anthony?"

Jim smiled once more. Another question from the past.

"You're right. Let's look closer. Perhaps a chemical that was added enabled the ashes to take on that form."

"I was thinking the same thing, if anything because some of those lines indicate incredibly exotic elements. See? I recognize those lines as iridium."

Jim was impressed. "It's not often to find someone who's memorized spectrography for such uncommon elements."

"Thank you, Mr. Anthony. But as you know, iridium comes primarily from space. And while my doctorates are in medicine and chemistry, I do have a Bachelor's in anthropology. For my final project I decided to study a tribe that lives in the Congo."

Jim nodded. "And?"

"This tribe has an interesting tradition when it comes to things coming from the sky. They collect rainwater religiously, but have also been subjected to a variety of meteor showers. The meteors that they can recover are considered to be opposite to the rainwater, which is sacred to them. Thus, the meteors are viewed as cursed objects. Priests will take them to a certain cave, and dispose of them there. No one but the priests are allowed near the cave. Based on a story they told me about a sickness that came from one of these meteors, I believe that a radioactive meteor once landed near their village long ago and inspired a legendary fear of the things."

"And the iridium, then, would be extracted from the meteorites hidden in this cave."

"Yes."

There was a moment of silence as they both planned ahead. But Muamba broke it quickly.

"Anthony—Jim—I need to stay with these people...but I can get you co-ordinates for the village."

"I'd be much obliged, Dr. Muamba. Muteba."

And they shook hands once again.

They both hoped they would meet once more, as Jim was granted use of the military jeep from Lieutenant Stevens and set out. Yet both knew that they would be hearing about the other sometime soon, for the great individual miracles they would produce.

• • •

The Congolese border was about two hours to Buru's southwest, and Jim spared no speed in getting down there. Now he wore his jungle attire of tough hiking boots, khaki shorts and a short sleeve shirt of the same cotton material. The hear was oppressive by the wind sliding past the open window was welcomed. After the first hour he realized that the irritation he was feeling was directed towards himself, for not insisting that Dr. Muamba join him on the quest ahead. Not because he doubted his ability to follow the doctor's instructions, but because he was suddenly rather lonely. He had thought he would have been alone when during the Professor Meteon case, and yet he had still come across Maria Flores and her all-girl army. He felt, with his encounter with Muamba, that perhaps he'd been offered the same choice he'd had when he stumbled on Maria in Panama. And this time, he had foolishly rejected such a choice!

He had other contacts besides Tom. Perhaps Maria was available, but it was unlikely from what he'd last heard of her. (In particular, she was tracking down a corporate head from the States who bankrupted his own business when his practices unleashed abuse lawsuits, only to open an even shadier business in Chile.) Dawkins had been given a much-needed holiday. And his grandfather Mephito did not travel with him.

So often now were his thoughts preoccupied with his companions! And his morality. He was realizing that now, and that rose, non-coincidentally, with the rising of his sixth sense. Adrenaline flooded into him and he felt the breath of the fight-or-flight response in some incarnate form come close to the back of his neck.

When he reached the Congo—*that* was when they struck!

There was no warning when the motorcycles came crashing out of the jungle and onto the open road. Jim stepped on the gas, hoping that "military-grade" in this case indicated greater speed than whatever they had out in this corner of the world. When he saw the bikes of the masked bandits surrounding the truck, however, those hopes swiftly vanished. He recognized the model and they were also (now formerly) of the British military. Each of the bikers wore long sleeves, tall boots, thick gloves, and as noted, masks—crude wrappings covering their faces, and thick goggles. In their hands were a variety of weapons, some very pristine, and some rather cobbled together. For every one of the modern rifles they held (and three of them had them for there were six of them in all), there were also long knives, a cricket bat, and what appeared to be an Enfield Mark II revolver.

The truck was speeding at its absolute limit for this environment, and they were still neck-and-neck. Even before one of the attackers raised his rifle to fire at the truck's tires, Jim knew he was going to lose this ride. There were two sharp cracks: the first as the rifle fired, and the second as the tires tore themselves apart. The truck lurched forward, but the driver-side door was already open. Jim performed a flawless lunge out of the vehicle, and landed with a heavy impact on the jungle floor. As the truck spun out of control and crashed somewhere in the distance, the motorcyclists began to create a circle around the detective. One of them was aiming his rifle at the adventurer's chest!

Even with his body pummeled by shock, Jim's eyes locked onto the gloved finger that held the trigger. When there was the slightest hint of a twitch, he dove aside, and to his relief heard the bullets strike the tire of the motorcycle opposite the shooter. (This realization came with a belated sense of admiration for these men who could wield these weapons single-handedly.) The man cried out and was flung from his metallic steed, which, like the truck, crashed. He had been the holder of the cricket bat, and his weapon of choice flew into the air with its wielder.

Jim Anthony caught the sports-implement-turned-murder-mechanism, and just as another burst of fire came down on him, he went into a simultaneous lunge and throw. His calculations were perfect; the bullets missed while the bat didn't. The wooden rod wedged itself in the spokes of the knife-user's front wheel, which went front-over-end and lost the driver his weapons.

From his forward bound Jim landed on his hands, and turned this into a flip towards one of the machine-gunners. Jim wished he could see through those goggles, to witness the surprise of his target, as he pulled on the barrel of his rifle and dislodged him from his bike.

Three were down! The man with the knives and the one with the cricket bat were fleeing into the woods when they saw their foe's power un-chained as it was. The one with the machine gun evidently thought he had a better chance, and aimed it again at Jim. But evidently, he hadn't learned anything from the mistake of his comrade—for once again there was a jump, and Jim took out the wheels of two more of the cycles with the wasted bullets!

There were no gunners left mounted, save for the one with the curious antique pistol. One of the machine-gunners, as he stood, barked at this man: "Shoot him, damn you! Shoot him!"

Jim saw the man's hand shaking. He was thinking the same thing Jim was, about the gun. He pulled the trigger...

...and the barrel exploded.

The shock blew him off his bike and knocked him unconscious—or at least he pretended it did. Jim felt a strange pang of pity for the mercenary over the embarrassment he'd just suffered.

The one who'd spoken before then suddenly had his gun at Jim's head again, and he spoke once more: "This is the finish, you fool! I *won't* miss a..."

But before he could say "gain," Jim beat him by sheer speed. Blinking would have destroyed the image of the kick that took out the gunner's left ankle. He crumpled to the ground, and Jim whirled around and caught him. Burly assassins such as these were great to be used as bowling balls, as he'd shown time and time again.

One of the remaining two sidestepped at the last second, and yet his rifle was at an angle so that his grip on it was broken. He frantically knelt to retrieve it, but by that time, Jim was already towering over him.

"You're going to lead me to the cave where your master keeps his exotic minerals," Jim stated plainly. Though he didn't need a guide—what he really meant was that this man was to be his hostage.

At first the man didn't speak, and Jim briefly considered that these attackers weren't linked to the villain behind all this. But suddenly, he broke the silence. "V-very well."

Keeping his prisoner in his peripheral vision, he then went about the task of finding a motorcycle that could still run. Thus satisfied, he angled it down the line of the road.

"You're on the back," Jim said then. "But try anything, and you'll get a swift reminder of who's driving."

The man did not reply. But like the man with the pistol, Jim could see his hands shake.

Eventually any trembling he had was lost when they were once again going down the road. A road which was no longer smooth to Jim—how he missed his truck!

• • •

It was only an hour or so more till they reached Dr. Muamba's coordinates. At once, Jim could tell that there was a degree of inaccuracy to the good doctor's instructions. He had been led instead to the village of the people who hid the meteorites that had possibly been used to create the unique "plastic ash" of the Buru crater. Within the village he could certainly find a guide, he realized. But his danger sense was burning hot. He noticed immediately there was no one outside of the many huts that comprised the village—and that was a warning sign for him. He hoped abandoned villages weren't becoming a motif for him.

And yet behind, he heard a gasp, even as his sixth sense pulsed. He turned around, and saw that his passenger was almost silently toppling off the back of his motorcycle. With a certain horror, Jim's eyes caught a glimpse of a tiny dart in his neck—one so similar to those used by Maria Flores. But as he quickly stepped off the cycle, Jim was able to assess in seconds that this one was more harmful than those of the Spanish beauty—there was no pulse. So much for a hostage. But Jim truly didn't mean for this man to *die*...!

Still, if he didn't move, he'd likely be dead too. He broke into a weaving run towards the village, furiously sweeping his eyes around to try to spot the killer who had shot his prisoner. Yet this was to no avail—likewise, he was unable to locate any villagers within the hut. When he reached the village's center, marked by a fire-pit filled with ashes, he heard the near-silent sound of a trigger being pulled. It was nearby, but with his reflexes flooding his brain, leaving space for nothing else, he couldn't place where it was exactly. Panting, he tried to scan again, when he heard the trigger once again. Because he was landing from his previous jump, he felt the dart's needle bury into his calf. Gasping, he tore it from his body, but evidently the toxin was affecting him anyway...

At this point he was used to being drugged. The villain he sought was a chemist, after all, having presumably had some sort of role in the Flame Wizard's creation of Greek fire, Baron Sturm's use of a hallucination-causing substance, and Professor Meteon's invention of a body-warping fog, among some others. So this poison, which was causing his vision to bulge and twist and be flooded with what looked like film scratches, was some-thing he could work past. He just hoped he wouldn't collapse dead like the other dart-victim—in a slower, and perhaps thus more painful, death!

Nonetheless, he had to question his reality when he saw the ashes in the fire-pit begin to stir and move. As they churned, beginning to form what Jim swore was a humanoid figure, he saw that a pistol of sorts was mixed in with the ashes. It had to have been the gun that fired the darts! It was upon reminding himself of the message in the crater that he saw there could be reality in the ashes shooting him. Now, the animate ashes were forming a shape so uncannily similar to a person. These ashes were of that living plastic as well—but of a clearly more advanced variety. Something that behaved like conditioned insects working in hormonal tandem. That didn't mean that hormones moved the plastic, but the individual ashes reminded Jim of large black bees.

The churning mass was able to strike fear into Jim once it became "hu-man." Indeed, it would have scared anyone, for these living ashes attempt-ed to form a "face"; and it failed miserably in this regard! The "eyes" were only dark pits that occasionally opened into full tunnels that went all the way through the monstrosity's head. Within the ashes was a low rum-bling—a detail that Dr. Muamba had perhaps missed in the chaos of the scene he'd been attending to. Suddenly the toxin weakened him further, and he lost this rumbling sound as his ear seemed to pop.

It had happened so suddenly—he'd lost, really, truly lost. But the hope of escaping final defeat wasn't gone from him yet. There was no time for a plan. Jim Anthony was good at working without them, a master. He had his reflexes to blame for that. He lunged forward into the cloud that walked like a man, and that phony face almost seemed to reflect surprise. He expected it to fire again, with the dart that would kill him, but didn't.

His vision went dark when he hit the cloud, and it went dark in two stages. First the dark soot made of plastic blocked out everything he could see, as its weight surrounded his face. Then, as the toxin burrowed deep-er into him, even that darkness was consumed by shadow, as he finally passed out.

• • •

Jim Anthony was surprised that he awoke at all. He had never slept like that before, and ached all over from stiffness. He must have tensed up as his body worked the venom through his system. He had indeed saved himself when his lightning fingers had plucked out the dart before it stayed in his flesh for too long. But he would be almost helpless for awhile due to the sharp pains that wracked him. For a fleeting, panicking moment he wondered if the poison *wasn't* out of his system, and death still waited for him. Yet he also knew he had the strength to survive. He just had to get moving.

It was still dark, but that was not alarming for him. He was in a cave, and above him were a few oil lanterns that burned bright. His eyes adjusted quickly to the new light conditions, which was reassuring. What was not inspiring, however, was the thinness of the air.

He must have been placed rather far below the ground for the air to be this scarce. But ahead of him was a tunnel with stairs leading both up and down—as well as a hallway going straight. He began to realize that he was in some sort of maze...

Then he looked up, and saw a great many bridges stretching here and there into more and more pathways.

It was like being in a giant beehive. (Evidently bees were on his mind. But they were such fascinating creatures, with the diversity amongst them creating the occasionally mysterious-seeming queens.) The only way for Jim to get out of here was to go up. For only darkness was below.

He could look over the ledge of the bridge that led to the hall and stairs. There were fewer lanterns down there, but he could still tell that the passages went ever, ever deeper. It was imposing to him. There were many things that could be down there—all kinds of monsters. Human and otherwise. And as he realized that his hope of finding a monster of the former category was down below, he knew which way on the stairs he was going.

Yet when he was across the bridge, he swore he could hear noises coming from up the stairs. They sounded to him like whimpers of torment—and he could scarcely ignore them. He sprinted up the stairs, not knowing what to expect.

But all the same, he was not surprised by what he encountered. In this carved stone room, there were a number of thick-barred cages where a variety of Africans were being kept. They were likely the villagers who had used these caves to dispose of the meteorites. Jim saw that there were doors on the cages, and the keys to these doors had been left behind.

Many of the villagers spoke in a language which Jim Anthony admittedly did not speak. But there were a few among them who cried out his name. "We've heard of you!" they said, in heavily accented English. "We never could have hoped that you would help us."

"I'm glad I could help," Jim replied.

"Please, we must escape quickly!" an older man said. He appeared to be a leader figure of some kind. "If we don't, we'll certainly all be killed."

"They didn't blindfold us, Jim Anthony," a younger man said. He had a marked resemblance to the older man, as well as a woman who stood close to the older man. "We saw the passage we were led down. We can easily return to the surface! You can come with us!"

Jim thought for only a second. "I can't go with you. I think the man I seek is here. At the very least, I must search for clues. I can get out by myself—you should escape while you can. Please, I beg you, do not argue."

They did argue at first, but Jim was resolute. And under the orders of the old man, they broke away from the detective to hurriedly retreat from the hive-like structure.

Jim was alone, but he was glad to have helped.

He went back down the stairs and descended, making sure to take a lantern as he did so. He would need it further below. He swiftly discovered that some parts of the passage had stairs, whereas some didn't—the architecture could be best described as chaotic. But Jim did not feel as if this randomness detracted from the intelligence of his fatal foe, for the unpredictable layout was not the product of lazy design—rather, the chaos was a matter of psychological warfare, dedicated at scrambling the minds of smart and tactical foes. If nothing was consistent in how the place was built, how could strategy arise within it? A military force would be hard-pressed in here if there were other defenses, as they could be easily surrounded. And for Jim, thinking randomly was occasionally difficult, as it meant shucking off his years of training.

And so it was that he went deep, deep down—so far down that if he lost his lantern, he could not rise again. So deep down the air was like ice, and indeed the soil and stone that he felt around him felt stiffened by this cold.

It would be a long and unpleasant descent. And the cold, growing stronger and stronger the deeper he went, made him think of Dante.

• • •

When Jim heard growling deep within the tunnels, he was almost glad. The descent swiftly became monotonous with no Virgil to talk to. His eyes were now like those of a cat—greyscale tunnels, bridges, and stairs around him were clear even beyond the color-bearing light of the lantern. His fighting capacity would be diminished without the lantern but not lost entirely. When he was this close to final victory, he could fight by sound if necessary; if he was deafened, the motion of his enemy in the air around him would be his guide. He was not going to let this villain escape, and the snarls in the dark did not dissuade him.

As always, his courage was his power. Upon reaching the third floor down from the level of the prison cell, he found that one of the staircase chambers was not as empty as the others—in the center was a small phonograph playing the growling noises over speakers. There was nothing there at all.

For a few flickering moments, Jim felt relief. In fact, he almost felt pity for the villain he tracked, because of how pathetic that gamble had been!

Yet upon stepping out onto the bridge he was confronted by something *else* that had a growl. He was expected to be scared away, or otherwise tricked into believing there was no living source behind the sound—only to be set upon by a genuine guard! Nature had chosen for this guard to make this sound, rather than an artificial recording set by a human hand. It looked prehistoric, and to see it down in the primordial darkness of a cave was only logical to Jim. It was the last living specimen of a saber-toothed tiger!

It hadn't been too long since Jim had had to wrestle with gigantic predators. To see this specimen in the flesh was still a shock, and presented a moral dilemma involving the fact that if he was forced to kill this beast, he'd be driving a species extinct. But he also had to stop millions of human lives from being interfered with, perhaps snuffed out. So instead, he decided to take a shortcut away from the beast: he jumped over the edge of the bridge, and planned to land on one of the bridges below.

He did this in the dark and with faith beside him—but he only put stock in faith when he knew he didn't really need it! His feet contacted the bridge safely and he was still able to hold onto his lantern. The cat's growl easily muted the recorded one, and the growl intensified briefly to Jim—before he was able to turn and see the cat lunge down and knock off him off this new bridge.

They fell down at least *two* more floors before they hit a bridge again, and obviously, they hit this one much harder. Jim was pinned below the tiger, and thus took most of the blow, but he was undeterred! The cat's titular saber fangs were about to gouge into him when he caught the creature by its furry throat. It was stunned and thus relented briefly in its assault, and that surprise was all Jim needed to push it back. Soon he was the one who had it pinned, and it snarled and hissed impotently at him as he restrained it. Yet it had the strength of the great cats, and one of its legs was able to shove back the fettering wrist. Jim lost his balance and had to back away as the claws came at his face—yet in jumping backwards to escape, he lost the lantern, which fell clattering into the still-deep pits below. He'd have to make good on his previous self-confidence...!

The creature's constant shrieking growl was good at betraying where it was in the dark. Plus, the cat eyes reflected the remaining ambient light from above, however faintly. He could work with that. When it tried to tackle him, he slid underneath it, swinging his legs up to catch the feline's underbelly and cause it to misplace its jump. Jim got back up on his legs, but so did the prehistoric beast. Its savage roar was the emblem of its other-world, a world opposed to the scientific modernity of Jim's own.

When they were facing each other again, the big cat once again lunged. But Jim heard its legs rush through the air, and thus could sense the outline of its shape. With perfect precision he caught the wrists of the creature's front legs, and was shoved back when it landed—though he held his ground. The tiger was forced to stand on its hind legs in an awkward position. Jim could very easily shove the creature over from here—and he'd have to move fast in any case should the creature decide to use its tusks on his wrists.

"I'm sorry, my friend."

A quick jerk to the right, and the howling extinct beast fell into the depths below.

Jim had no idea how the beautiful, terrible thing had survived, but it was wrong that the master of this hive-fortress had turned it to his cause. Though just one animal had died, an entire species had just been exterminated. Jim wondered if perhaps this was a coded warning. At the bottom of this shift sat a mind that could make humanity as emblematic of the distant past as a saber-toothed cat.

Up above, the cheap recording continued, in pale imitation of the real thing. A simple trap, that—intended only to stop invaders easily, one way or another. It had indeed partially caught Jim Anthony, but it had not killed him as it would another man. And it worked in stages—the most unprepared would be driven away by the suspense of hearing the growl. Those who got closer, being braver but still mortal, would be distracted by their joy of learning the growl was only a recording. And then they would be mauled.

There would be more sophisticated snares ahead. He had no idea what, but he would have to find out.

He hoped that he would live to see color again. Having to see in the dark was upsetting after a while.

• • •

When Jim Anthony was down another two or three floors, he at once began to sense danger once again—and it wasn't just from the pain in his lungs, or the fact that it was starting to feel like ice was actually forming down here, making the bridges all the more perilous. There were still some stray photons bouncing around down here, as Jim could occasionally see the white ghosts of his breath as he walked.

He stopped, and let his ears probe ahead—his fingers ran against the wall to see if there were any telling vibrations. Sure enough, there was something lumbering through the passage, notably weightier than even the prehistoric tiger. In this weight it was slower, and Jim at once hoped that that also meant clumsier, and easier to pitch over the edge. Based on sound, the thing was still in the distance, and Jim wanted to cover as much ground as he could before he was forced to fight.

But to his surprise, the hub ahead of him, surrounded by walls on all sides (unlike the bridges), did not simply stretch into another naked bridge. Instead, there was merely one staircase, and it led down into actual rocky tunnels. Everything else had been the hubs forming columns down a gigantic central shaft. The *machinery* that would have been needed to construct this place...!

Machinery was on his mind as he got closer and closer to the heavy footsteps, which, if the sensation in his hair was correct, was jarring loose some soil above his head. He didn't want to think about being in the dark if any part of these caves collapsed. Well-constructed they were indeed, but these deeper portions had a heavier quantity of rock on them. And nothing man-made was perfect.

Which was good, because his coming foe was a machine.

Suddenly, he felt the air open up ahead of him—he was no longer descending a cramped staircase, but was instead in a larger room. A quick study of the outer wall indicated the room was likely circular. There was a gap in this circular wall up ahead, from which the definitively mechanical thing was hauling itself. As it slowly entered the room that Jim found himself calling an arena, he could tell that whatever it was, it had four legs, likely giant pistons—and he could pick out the sound of hissing steam, suggesting that was what it was powered by. The rest of its appearance he couldn't guess at, but it almost certainly had weapons. The shape of the room meant that this was where he and the machine would fight. And once the loud clanking stopped, leaving only the sound of escaping steam—there were flashes in the night! Orange-hot flashes—from twin mounted machine guns!

Whatever steered this metallic beast was not prepared for Jim to already be in motion when it fired—he was several yards away from where the bullets struck. But the guns did not stop, and automatically tracked the fleet-footed detective as he bounded along the rim of the fighting ring. Jim kept an eye on it even as he bolted, observing finally that the mechanical warrior's four legs were connected to a plate of steel—and atop that was a large metal box upon which the guns were mounted. Several eye-like sensors were mounted within the box, evidently still dependent on visible light to see. Yet the belts coming off the guns were enormous. They were the suppliers of light for the machine, as well as death for its target. Evidently the difficulty of fighting in the dark was worth blinding the machine outside of its own gunfire.

But again, this trap was built for one who was not Jim Anthony. Jim could dance around bullets, especially when they were being fired from a stiff, brainless machine. Albeit a sophisticated one! For suddenly, the steam was shrieking like a tea-kettle, and the guns ceased providing illumination. Instead, the piston legs pushed the titanic slaughter-machine forward in a terrific charge! Jim intended to escape through the door from which his enemy had come, and fused this act with the straining dodge necessary to evade the charge. The entire cavern shook as tons of steel crashed against the wall.

Jim also hit the wall, or rather, the door. He hadn't been able to see that a hermetic seal had come down over the exit, and presumably the entrance as well, as he'd been concentrating on the machine's movement. The impact was painful and stunning, but the metal beast was also disabled by its dive. Still, perhaps it was not as awkward as Jim believed it was—once he was on his feet he knew he'd have to be on the move again, but suddenly, the guns blazed, and he felt a fiery scratch against his calf. A bullet had gotten him! He could tell that it hadn't actually burrowed into the flesh, instead merely grazing him, and the adrenaline was smothering the pain, but it caused him to fall. A swift roll dodged the next burst of gunfire—sizzling scars were left in the floor beside his shoulder! He managed to stand again, but the orange light vanished. The machine was going to charge him again!

A plan formed in the detective's mind in less than a second, and in a similar fractional moment, he put it into action. A slide across the stone floor carried him under the belly of the machine, and a deafening crash came as it collided with the wall once more. When he jumped onto his target's backside, he felt his leg crackle with pain, and it hurt his hands to seize the rough metal of the central box of its body. As his hands fumbled in the darkness, they brushed against the pipe that vented the steam, and he cried out in pain as his fingers were burnt. But he knew he had to locate the source of the steam, because that would be the thing's weak point. Remove a beast's heart and its blood ceases to flow.

The pipes led towards a box, wherein his ears could hear the source of steam—but this box, too, was blazing hot. He had to move fast—he was close enough to the guns to see their shape, and to see that they were turning to face him. His sweatshirt was torn anyway, so it was a simple matter to tear it to shreds, and then to ball those shreds and shove them within the steam-pipes. There was barely enough to clog the burning apertures, but he figured this would do it.

He jumped off of the giant clanking thing, and it slowly turned to face him. But to Jim's overt shock, he saw the fabric catch on fire. That should be impossible—the water in the steam would soak the cloth and prevent the convection from the pipes from spawning a blaze. And yet, with the new light from the fresh fires, he saw that the machine had simply opened auxiliary vents in its front, which also began to release vapor. They definitely hadn't been there before. Jim shouldn't have been surprised that his enemy could adapt like this, but he was, which impressed him.

The guns blazed again, creating a ballet of shadows between their strobe and the new light from tatters of his shirt burning away. By now he was used to evading the slightly-slow tracker, but the real challenge came from loosening his belt once again while in the midst of backing off.

He did it at last, when the machine had to let its guns cool. Without fear he approached the machine, and cracked his belt-whip just twice. Each time the weighted buckle crushed metal cylinders. By striking at the right angle with the right amount of force, Jim was able to close the pipes. Even as the fabrics in the pipes crumbled to dark ashes, he could tell that there wasn't a third set of vents.

The guns began to fire again, and once again Jim was on the move. But within moments, deep within the machine, he could hear metal straining from a great internal pressure. He got as far from the thing as possible, and the strain rose into cracking, and from there...

...Jim cried out in shock when the machine burst—not because any pieces of it hit him, but because he had become so reliant on his hearing that the explosion seemed unnaturally loud. He was significantly shaken, but he could walk. That was all that mattered.

In the dark, he could hear the hermetic doors opening. He had retained

...the guns did not stop...

his sense of direction all throughout the fight, and so he went deeper into the belly of the beast.

• • •

Jim Anthony never thought he'd have gratitude for downhill stairs. But the truth was he was fairly beaten up. Bruises were rising, and it felt like some things in his arm and chest were broken. Hopefully nothing more serious than that. Nothing to neutralize him completely.

When he reached the bottom of the stairs, the echoes of his breath coming back to him gave him an odd image. The walls appeared to be arranged in almost random patterns. He probed forward with his fingers, missing the brief moment of light he'd had while engaging the mechanical killer. When he felt the walls ahead of him his worst fears were confirmed. He had come across a true maze, and again, there were no lights.

He would have to feel his way along. If he had his equipment, he would perhaps have phosphorous powder that he could use to mark the way (and he could do a lot with that, actually). For now he would have to work with what he had, which was just what he'd been doing this whole time.

The silence of the cave-complex, which was seeming more and more like the stillness of a tomb, was at its worst in this maze. There was a sense of claustrophobia in the air, even though Jim typically didn't suffer from such a terror. Not only was there the possibility of becoming permanently imprisoned in the maze, but there was also the possibility of traps—and other things—being hidden in the shadows. Here was only cruel death for Jim Anthony.

Still, he was having an optimistic sense of progress. Mazes were rarely alike, but he had had to travel through many before, albeit none in the state he was in now, with the environment he was in now. With experience came expertise, however slightly. So he was something of a maze expert.

Except in his brain, he wasn't calling this a maze. He was calling it a labyrinth, and every time the word washed over him he felt a chill. For in the stories of things specifically called labyrinths, there was always also—a minotaur.

He debated the possibility of such a beast actually existing. He wouldn't put it past his foe to create something like it—a horrid perversion of science binding the man and the bull. Yet a creature like that would be noticeable. If Jim could sense the approach of his last opponent, a heavy monster like the minotaur would also betray its vibratory or auditory presence. He was alone in the labyrinth, and he didn't know if that improved the situation or not.

Suddenly, behind him, he thought he heard someone sigh.

He turned around hurriedly, despite not being able to see. (He started to remember there was a hard limit on how long human eyes could be exposed to darkness before they simply ceased to work. He *would* have to get out of it soon.) But he realized the sigh was possibly a hallucination—he'd had a lot of those lately, it seemed, and so he was able to remain calm about the fact that he had this one. In any case, sensory deprivation often created such delusions. And something as minor as a sigh was...

Jim Anthony suddenly cried out in pain. Something was raking sharp nails across his chest! His shirt was torn and flesh cut.

He backed up against a wall, but could feel a passage to his right. He bolted down it, but the sigh that he heard was steadily becoming a mighty rush of wind, as if a tornado was creating itself out of raw malice. Again the unseen claws lashed out, and deep cuts formed on the detective's backside. Even though he could feel the presence of this thing—the labyrinth's minotaur—so very close to him, he could not see it. He swung out a couple of cheap punches, and yet connected with nothing. There was just a slightly cold patch of air—one which could tear at the detective's flesh with a deadly malice!

As he traveled down a long passage, Jim decided to cease his hesitation and fight with full force, hopeful that his foe was not as intangible as it initially seemed. And yet, as he retreated, he became afraid—for none of his blows were connecting. Yet new wounds appeared all over his body, and he could feel blood drip down his forehead and torso.

There was only one way to stop this wraith, and that was to outrun it. But as Jim broke into a sprint, he slammed swiftly into a wall. The maze, suddenly, became like a nightmare to him, and a cold sweat broke out all over his tanned body. His breathing became ragged, and even a man of his resolve had to fight to hold down a terrified scream.

He had hung onto his orientation, however, and assuming that the escape from the labyrinth lay opposite to where he had entered, he slowly worked his way along the walls, while also trying to escape the agonizing slashes inflicted upon him. Jim Anthony was weakening fast.

His heart nearly stopped when he reached a dead end. It seemed useless to go on. But sentiment came upon him, a subconscious preservation method—he saw in his head the face of all his companions, and of his family: his living grandfather Mephito, and his late parents, Fawn Johntom and Shean Boru Anthony. Sometimes, at the very edge of mortality, Jim would find that even these images couldn't save him. His hopelessness was too strong. And yet now, those faces *did* aid him in that darkness—for after all, their power was to make his burden lighter, as an ability rested within all of their great talents.

Once he was out of the dead end, he began to regain confidence in his orientation—the walls and corners began to yield to him. Behind him, that strange low rushing wind seemed to intensify, but he took that as encouragement: it was likely that the presence was cursing his closeness to escape. He *had* to believe that was the case. He had to believe that he would thwart his enemy's idle threats of vengeance.

His sensitive eyes began to catch some faint changes in his surroundings. He didn't dare to hope that they were light rays—he realized then the depth of his fear of dying here. But he ran towards this light, and it did indeed intensify. Jim had managed to extract himself again—yet the spectre was still not done with him.

Even in the light it had no shape—at least, none that Jim could tell, from restarting his assault on the thing. He was still blind—once the light had come upon him fully; his weakened eyes were full of blazing agony. But he was able to suppress the pain through sheer will, and he knew at once that his only hope would be to keep running. The lights provided illumination for a descending staircase. How far below the Earth could this complex go?

More slashes lashed out at him as he escaped. But eventually, he realized several long moments had passed wherein he was not attacked. The rushing, also, had slowly faded away; only his ragged breath echoed in the bright passage. He stopped, and slowly turned around. His eyes were finally adjusting to the light, though the pain tainted everything with a red glow. There was nothing behind him but the darkness of the maze.

Of course, he had no idea if there had ever been anything back there at all.

The villain he'd tracked here—and he hoped he was close to him tremendously—had been the one who had been responsible for his recent hallucinations. He could have easily used a nigh-undetectable gaseous drug. And yet, Jim was entirely convinced that if he ran chemical tests on the air of the labyrinth, he would find nothing.

He didn't care that he would never know what the minotaur had been.

It was probably better he didn't.

• • •

The stairs went down quite a ways, and eventually transitioned from their original form—being carved from stone—to a passage lined with metal fashioned into art deco ornaments. But it wasn't entirely that style. It was much plainer than that, much more efficient, and yet it suggested prestige besides the shabby look of the rest of this gargantuan subterranean system. This place was near its king, and therefore it deserved some decoration, however slight.

There was no doubt in Jim's mind. This was the finish. He had reached the heart of the matter, of the labyrinth he'd been trapped in that was so much larger than the one he'd just escaped.

At long last, he could see a door. It was of a Victorian fashion, but had been worn by many decades. Jim's hand was shaking when he placed it on the cold iron knob. But the door flung open, and he stepped inside.

The room seemed simple enough. He saw oak-panel walls, and an enormous mahogany desk, upon which sat a variety of scientific instruments from a wide range of fields. There was a cramped-looking bed in the corner with silk sheets, and a simple-looking electric lamp which faintly lit the room. Near the door was a large jar or urn of some kind. The color of the rug, and of the paint on the ceiling, were both a deep crimson. Or rather, patches of red mixed with patches of dirt brown. Dirt...

"Yes, dirt," came a voice suddenly.

Jim Anthony jumped. He must have said the word aloud, but he didn't remember his lips moving. He didn't want to consider that the holder of that voice could hear his thoughts. He turned to look at the source of the voice.

Sitting in a wheelchair was a beautiful woman. Her brown hair was very short, almost as if it had been just a few weeks since she had been completely bald. The story behind this hair was perhaps linked to the long string of crimson scars going down the right side of her face. Some of these scars touched the edge of her right eye, and there was some discoloration in the white and part of the pupil. She had a serious face, lined with many years spent hard at work. Her right arm was shrunken somewhat compared to her left, and both her legs were similarly dwarfed.

"Dirt is what we are now, Jim Anthony. So far below the surface, there is no logic or meaning, for no civilization but that which I've created could exist down here. And because I am the mother of that society, I decree what is logical and meaningful. Neither of us have meaning, for I spit in the face of meaning! Meaning was taken away from me when I was born. Before I even cried, I was set on this path."

Jim feigned confusion. "I don't understand. Who are you?"

"Jim Anthony, do not condescend to me. You know who I am, in spirit, at least. I am worthy of your respect. Moreso, I believe, than anyone else who has faced you before."

"You clearly respect yourself greatly. Why do you need any extra from me?"

"I respect myself because I worked to make it to this tier of power. I am wise enough to recognize when I have made proper and professional decisions in my life. And I have strong knowledge of my weaknesses as well as my strengths—that is certainly more important knowledge." Then she paused. "Do you know *your* weaknesses, Jim Anthony?"

"Who are you?" Jim repeated then.

"I am Dr. Tara Stanrocca. You won't find any records of my attendance at the universities of the world—I had them destroyed. Not the universities, that is to say—well, I shouldn't speak so soon. I have always made sure to stay in the shadows, and there are no greater shadows than where the sun doesn't reach. At the center of the Earth."

She began to wheel herself towards him, and Jim saw that she was clad in a brown dress perhaps made of sackcloth. He could see now, in better light, a deeper truth in her face, the truth behind her seriousness. She had the faint trace of a smile, which was the child entirely of pride. It wasn't that she wasn't aware of her pride—it's that she *was*, and that knowledge only made her prouder.

Jim Anthony saw no difference in gender, though he recognized there were differences. The circumstances that drove the life of the woman sitting before him would have grounds in how society treated women compared to men—male dismissal of the significance of femininity could have driven her to her present career. And yet a genius of her well-demonstrated pedigree should have been able to find respect among all save the most diehard of misogynists. No, this had been a choice for her.

Once again, she took his breath away when she began talking—talking in that knowing way that suggested that tendrils from her brain reached into the depths of his. "Oh, the scar?" she said suddenly. "I got that last year." Jim had been wondering about the scar (and she had probably been watching his eyes as he scanned it)—he had considered that she had been disfigured and without her feminine beauty, she had become evil. But that was clearly not the case now if her words were true. She had been like this long before her features were damaged...

"A bit of a lab accident at one of my former bases," she continued. "It's good that I lost that one—the security was dreadful, and you might have found it while looking for Kallinikos! I was assisting the Flame Wizard in creating Greek fire when his clumsiness caused my injury. I gave him an intelligence-limiting drug as a punishment, and that's why you defeated him.

"A component of that same drug was borrowed by Meteon when he made his gas, and it was modified using extracts of various fungi and flowering herbs to make the hallucinogen that the Baron Sturm employed."

"You willingly admit to having employed those murderers."

"There's no point in denying it. After all, I will kill you."

"I don't believe—"

"*NO,*" she said then. "*I* will *kill you.*"

The air hung with a tense silence.

"You will not interrupt my plans any further. There's no point in delaying." And she whipped her good arm down suddenly, and from her sleeve came a handgun. She pointed it at Jim and fired.

Once again, it must be noted that Jim Anthony had trained himself to react at the very sound of a pulled trigger. He jumped and twisted in the air, but Stanrocca had aimed accordingly, and Jim cried out as the bullet grazed his temple. The pain caused him to land improperly, and he was stunned for several moments. During this time Stanrocca aimed the gun at a jar she had standing next to the door. She shot it at the base and the porcelain shattered like glass. Inside was a pile of grey dirt. Yet it did not remain in a pile for long.

In a grotesque perversion of intelligence, the bundle of soil stirred just as Anthony did. When the detective saw what was happening he was reminded of the ashes in the village, which had become the monster that had brought to the cave to begin with. "This is indeed what I've been doing with the iridium that was originally abandoned here, before I made some enhancements to the original structures created inside the cave by the natives. An element as rare as iridium has quite a few tricks up its sleeve."

The dirt had become a bulky humanoid figure, with the same uncanny lack of features as the automaton Jim had engaged on the surface. It tried to form a face, but mercifully gave up quickly. Like its master, it definitely seemed to lack patience.

Jim Anthony lacked patience too! He rushed the monstrosity...

...but the arm of the titanic creature swung out, and he found himself on the stairs—severely concussed. If his bones weren't broken already, they were now. He played back the punch in his mind, and saw that the creature had a tremendous advantage over him. It could route all of its mass into its blows, briefly sacrificing its shape and balance to send what must have truly been several hundred pounds of force outwards. He was lucky to be alive.

The creature was upon him again, its gelatinous form almost galloping like a rabid dog. He stabbed outward with a tough kick, but it did no good. The mass was able to form around it, and now suddenly it had his leg. With two awkward chops at the tube of dirt that clutched his calf, he managed to disrupt the mass enough to yank his leg loose. He rolled to roll away but the churning swarm pounced on him. Now it was a blanket that anchored his legs *and* his arms to the floor.

Dr. Stanrocca wheeled over to him, and her smile was only slightly more visible. "So sad. When I watched you face down my three servants, I saw a glimmer of something as good as myself. So sad."

"You...were watching...?" Jim gasped. The blanket of earth was slowly pushing down on him, squeezing life out of him like a python. "How? I... would have spotted...cameras..."

"Who said I needed cameras?" Stanrocca retorted. "I know what you were thinking as you went through the maze—or rather, should I not know, I can deduce it. You were wondering about the minotaur in there. Was what the minotaur? Perhaps it was from another world, one which lies beyond the barriers of science. Perhaps I have powers from such a world. You wouldn't be the *first* to call me a witch, Jim Anthony! I..."

"You've been lonely, haven't you?" Jim said then. "The others ranted because they were emotionally unbalanced. But you're wiser than they— you've kept your passions in check. And yet even the most brilliant minds can't stave off a desire for companionship. In fact, the smarter one gets, the lonelier one feels in that regard...trust me. And so now you're a little shaky, aren't you? Because it's been so long since you've had even a near-equal to explain these things to..."

"Yes. But you've lost. You are clearly no equal of mine." And she was leaning forward somewhat as she said that. Jim grinned, and in response she leaned farther forward. "What's so funny?" And his smile got wider.

"If you were watching me during the Baron Sturm case, you would re-call that I sent an invention of mine into a subterranean canal that linked Sturm to a site in San Francisco, where he intended to trap and kill me. That drone was able to broadcast a radio signal through water and stone alike back to me."

"That is correct. I was not impressed by that. My own developments in radio waves and electromagnetic radiation in general, are far superior."

"I don't doubt it. But I've been improving the signal, so much so that I doubt anything can block it. The device can be tracked anywhere in the world, even within it. If I were to have one of these bugs on me, anyone with one of my trackers could find me no matter what."

"You are speaking with a fool's desperation, Anthony. I had my ash-man strip you of anything of value, save your belt so that you could have a fighting chance. No matter how small the bug was, it is gone now—gone to China, in fact! If your friends track it, they will find a trap waiting for them. A pack of mercenaries aided by a pair of my plastic-particle creations. They will be torn apart."

And at those words, suddenly, Jim became very pale. Stanrocca could see that he was envisioning what she had described: the gristly destruction of his friends and allies. He could see that it brought her great pleasure.

"Speaking of people being ripped apart, Jim Anthony," she continued. "Perhaps I could compare your brain to those of other geniuses who have crossed my path...after I've removed it from your cadaver. I've been very interested in where intelligence comes from, being of such obvious status myself. It would be nice if I could perhaps use my research to chemically or therapeutically increase my potential for knowledge. I think I will take your brain from you, however, while you are still living and awake. You're right, I have been lonely. But I will compensate for past solitude with the music of your screams."

There was no emotion to her voice as she spoke this—the egomania that wracked her could only be found in the rawness of the words she used.

The creature that pinned Jim began to rearrange itself, shaping some of its volume into the sharp instruments it would presumably use to split open the detective's skull. The sharpness of the blades was as precise as the smoothness of the letters which had brought Jim to Africa. He was visibly shaking in fear as he saw these blades. But suddenly, the fear washed away, and knowingly, he made eye contact with the scientist in the wheelchair. His face had become one of smugness!

Stanrocca only realized what had happened *after* Jim had ripped his way out of the beast!

She had let her lust for violence overtake her. It grew wild on seeing a theatrical imposture of defeat and terror—it was her weakness to witness that in her victims. By altering its mass the creature had shifted away its weight from Jim's arms. With the entire thing upon him, he couldn't move, but it had given him a brief opening and he'd taken it. If she had just let it crush him that would be the end of it all!

When Jim Anthony was on his feet, he began a series of lithe dodges to make sure the creature never seized him again. "Your arrogance was natural, of course—I ensured it by taking a second bug along," Jim explained. "When you got rid of the first one you were sure you'd isolated me and killed my friends on top of it! But you didn't know that I took another bug in my morning breakfast. Danger sense, remember? It seemed like the thing to do. And if those transmission waves can go through stone, they can definitely go through my stomach lining!"

"But there's still no chance of rescue! My traps are still out there! Your servants will never reach you in time. I have still won."

Jim only laughed. "I noticed that your legs are rather thin, Dr. Stanrocca—atrophied, to be precise! You truly haven't walked in years; that wheelchair isn't a prop in your play. Remember that to get all the way down here...one has to take the stairs."

Just then, an explosion wracked the room, and Stanrocca cried out in surprise. Through the wall came several figures led by the familiar face of Tom Gentry. Jim didn't recognize all the figures of the assorted men and women who had just arrived, but his friends around the world numbered in the thousands. However, though there were a blend of races on display, there was one man of African descent who stood out. It was, of course, Dr. Muteba Muamba.

"Sorry, we couldn't find a way to get the door open," Tom said, grinning. "Which figures, given that it was probably a secret, right?" His eyes lit up suddenly as he looked at his friend. "Jim! There's a passage back here, equipped with an elevator. We found a door to it hidden on the brush of the hill that the cave's main entrance opens out of. It had a puzzle-lock on it...I'll tell you about how it worked and how we solved it once we're out of here..."

Behind Jim, he could hear the sound of the particle-creature reforming. It had been disrupted by the shock-waves in the air from the explosion, but was once again a humanoid. Jim turned to face it.

"What in God's name is that, Anthony?" Dr. Muamba called out.

"It's made of the same synthetic material that spelled my name in the crater," Jim said calmly. "Tom, do you have a chemistry set with you?"

"Coming right up!" Tom turned back into the group, which extended back into the darkness of Stanrocca's access tunnel. "Sergeant Collins, pass it forward..."

"I'm going to need some of what our friend-in-science Conant calls the superacid."

Tom searched frantically in one of the packs he carried. The bottle containing the superacid was painted black, to indicate how dangerous it was.

"Everyone stand back! No one breathe the vapors!" Even Stanrocca, her face twisted with hatred, backed away.

Jim took the bottle, and upon unscrewing it, threw it towards the mass. He couldn't hit all of it while also escaping to a safe distance, but with a flash of smoke and what appeared to be a rumbling scream, it was mostly destroyed. Even the fumes rusted the metal it touched. If it weren't for the general size of the room, and the open air coming through the secret passage, the lungs and throats of all assembled would be burning.

As Jim stumbling, Tom cried out, "We planted explosives at both entrances to the shaft! We need to get out of here within five minutes! The blast will carry along the rock and wipe everything out."

Jim Anthony face suddenly flashed with surprise. He didn't exactly know why Tom had done that—but he remembered his own obsession with this case. Tom had seen it, and had interpreted it to mean that there were to be no chances taken with a villain such as Tara Stanrocca.

He considered abandoning that implied promise which he had made to him for the last few dreadful months, which said that the master villain of this and three other terrible incidents of crime should not be spared, not given a second chance. Human empathy wrestled with cold logic—the logic of stopping Stanrocca from hurting anyone ever again versus the empathy of giving her a chance to reform.

But he made a startling realization: that the mental battle that raged within him was akin to the physical one against Stanrocca and her forces. On her side was that icy calculation, and on Jim Anthony's was that stubborn, irrational humanity. He held his hand out to the wheelchair-bound queen-pin.

"Come with us. I'll carry you if I have to. You should face society's justice."

"I told you, Jim," Stanrocca said emphatically. "I hid down here, and became dirt, because I was something worse on the world above. I was an outsider on their terms, so I chose to become an exile of my own design." And suddenly, she took a glinting handgun from a pouch attached to the arm of her chair. "If you try to take me with you, you take away from me the freedom I've created for myself, and for that, I will shoot you."

"Dr. Stanrocca—"

"*NO*," she said then. She looked at the floor. "No. I *will* shoot you, even though you have overcome the weakness I have seen in you, whilst causing me to be consumed by mine. You are the stronger one here, and in respect of that, I offer to remove myself from the universe's equation. But be warned..." And her eyes were on his again. "If you fall to your weaknesses again and thus become weaker than I in death, you will have misfortune and dishonor laden upon you endlessly from my grave. You must keep your promises, and keep your world and everyone in it safe."

Jim had been feigning fear earlier, but as a parting gift, Tara Stanrocca had given it to him for real.

"Now go."

Jim said nothing, and he and his compatriots sprinted down the passage. Eventually they reached an elevator car which swiftly rocketed them back to a hidden door on the surface. Upon ascending the shaft, Jim's eyes had spotted the burning fuses of the explosives that would soon reduce the artificial base to a bitter memory.

And yet, the deafening explosion that concluded the detective's war on the Four Elements did not exceed the cavern, and nothing fell in. Far beneath, nigh-impossible architecture crumbled, and the unbelievable mind of one of the most wicked people to ever live was burnt away.

"It's over, Jim," Tom said. "It's all finally over."

"It began with fire, and it ended with fire," Jim said then. And his danger sense did not buzz—Tom was right. There was no menace here, only peace at last.

Some of that peace belonged to Stanrocca, whose superficial scars were never a problem next to those hidden beneath her skin. Jim quietly wished mercy upon her when she reached Judgment.

He gave a hearty sigh as he realized he would rest tonight, his troubles washed away. He could return to the sturdy ground of a world of order and peace, a world which he had forged for him. Yet as it always had and always would, the fire of this forge burned hot in him, pushing him to the next adventure...to the next terrific triumph.

Finis

ABOUT OUR CREATORS

AUTHOR –

ADAM MUDMAN BEZECNY - started writing nine years after the 1994 lab accident that created him. Seven years later he adopted the name and infinite creed of "Mudman." Since then he's summarily failed several destinies in White Bear Lake, Minnesota, and Morris, Minnesota. He's also experimented lovingly with filmmaking and film criticism. He first came in contact with the pulp world when Alan Moore and Kevin O'Neill's *The League of Extraordinary Gentlemen* introduced him in turn to the works of Philip Jose Farmer and the Wold Newton Universe. His true passion in writing, however, is telling stories of a Multiverse he's been creating for his entire life. Two stories of his Multiverse, the sci-fi/horror/fantasy/pronominal-nightmare piece *Dieselworld* and the blog-based horror invasion yarn *Words from the Inner Circle*, can be found at (http://dieselcascade.blogspot.com/2013/07/1.html) and (http://innercirclechats.blogspot.com/2014/05/introduction.html), respectively. His novel Deus Mega Therion is forthcoming soon from Odd Tales Productions, and his book Tail of the Lizard King has been published by Ramble House.

INTERIOR ILLUSTRATOR –

RICHARD JUN – is an aspiring comic book illustrator and a professional doctor of optometry. He spent most of his formative years poring over comics books. He carefully and meticulously copied the likes of Art Adams, John Buscema, John Byrne and Jim Lee. He majored in drawing and painting at Loyala University in Chicago and was awarded scholarship to attend summer classes at the Art Institute of Chicago. After graduation, Rich worked odd jobs but struggles to crack the art world

Keen at making his own way in the world independent from his parents, he went to graduate school to become an eye doctor. He ventured off to New York City for graduate school and loved every minute of it. Rich has spent the last ten years treating patients from eye diseases and preventing blindness. All the while, he continued his affair with comic book and action figures.

Rich lives in Madison, Wisconsin with his lovely girlfriend and two rescued pit bulls. One day while perusing the mail, they came across a comic book art class. She encouraged him to jump in and everything changed. Rich met his instructor, Jeff Butler, and continued to study with him for two years. Under Jeff's tutelage, his aspirations have reignited.

Rich is grateful and thrilled to work under the incredible Airship 27 banner with Ron Fortier and Rob Davis.

COVER ARTIST –

ADAM BENET SHAW –Accomplished painter, illustrator, and comics creator, Adam has garnered acclaim across a number of artistic media. After completing studies at the Cleveland Institute of Art in Ohio, the Edinburgh College of Art in Scotland and Watts Atelier in California, Shaw was selected as an emerging American artist to watch by European gallery owners and exhibited in London, England. He has been featured in "New American Painting", selected multiple times for the Arkansas Art Center's Delta Exhibit, and shown at the prestigious "Red Clay Survey" at the Huntsville Museum of Art. His work has also been shown in over 50 group and solo shows in the US and internationally. His figurative paintings are a prominent part of a 140-foot mural entitled "The History of Cotton" at the National Cotton Exchange Museum, St. Jude's Children's Research Hospital, the National Contact Bridge Museum, and a treasured part of private and corporate collections. He has created storyboards for several motion pictures, including Paramount Pictures' film "Black Snake Moan" directed by Craig Brewer, stage design for operas and corporate events, and character illustrations for the gaming industry. His published graphic novel work includes the series "Dead In Memphis", "Bloodstream" for Image Comics, "David: The Illustrated Novel" from Shepherd King Publishing and "Harpe: America's First Serial Killers" from Cave-in-Rock Publishing. He shares his love of art through teaching and workshops at his studio in the Broad Avenue Arts District in Memphis. Recently he has been painting book covers for pulp publishers Pro Se Productions and Airship 27 Productions.